GW01454245

TH
ANL

M.Sholokhov

THE FATE OF A MAN AND EARLY STORIES

Raduga Publishers Moscow

Translation from the Russian
Illustrated by *Boris Alimov*
Designed by *Pavel Nikiporets*

© Raduga Publishers 1989

Printed in the Union of Soviet Socialist Republics

ISBN 5-05-002338-6

CONTENTS

EARLY STORIES

"I was born in 1905... During the Civil War I was on the Don.

"I had joined the army in 1920 and served my time in the Don region. For a long time I was in the grain-procurement corps. We chased after the bands that roamed around the Don right up until 1922, and they chased after us..."

Mikhail SHOLOKHOV.
From his autobiography

THE BIRTH-MARK*

I

Empty cartridge cases still reeking of burnt cordite, a mutton bone, a field map, an operations report, a medallioned bridle that smells of horse sweat, and a loaf of bread. All that's on the table. And on a rough-hewn bench coated with mildew from the damp wall sits the squadron commander, young Nikolai Koshevoi, his back firmly lodged against the windowsill. There is a pencil between his numb, stiff fingers. Among the out-of-date posters spread over the table lies a half-completed form. The hairy scrap of paper states, *Koshevoi, Nikolai. Squadron Commander. Land Worker. Young Communist.*

Slowly the pencil traces the figure '18' beside the word 'age'.

Nikolai is broad in the shoulders and looks older than he really is. It's those creases at the corners of his eyes, and his old-mannish stoop, that age him.

'He's only a kid, a mere boy, a greenhorn,' they say jokingly in the squadron. 'But just try to find someone else who could wipe out two bandit gangs without hardly losing a man, and lead his squadron through six months of battles and skirmishing as well as any veteran.'

*English translation ©Progress Publishers 1975.

Ashamed of being only eighteen is Nikolai. His pencil always crawls to a standstill at that hated word 'age' and his cheeks flush with annoyance. Nikolai's father was a Cossack; and so is he, by right of birth. He remembers, almost as in a dream, how at the age of five or six his father lifted him on to his cavalry mount.

'Hang on to the mane, son,' he shouted. Nikolai's mother was smiling at him from the kitchen door, but her face paled as she stared at those little legs clamped over the horse's steep-sided back, and at his father holding the rein.

That was a long time ago now. Nikolai's father had disappeared in the war against the Germans and never been heard of since. His mother had died. From his father Nikolai had inherited his love of horses, a boundless valour, and a birth-mark like his father's on the left leg, just above the ankle, a mole as big as a pigeon's egg. Until the age of fifteen he led a hand-to-mouth existence as a farm-hand, then he got himself enlisted in a Red regiment that was passing through his village, put on one of their long greatcoats and went off to fight Wrangel.* One day in summer, when Nikolai was bathing in the Don with the Military Commissar, the Commissar said to him, stammering and jerking his shell-shocked head, and slapping Nikolai's stooped sun-blackened shoulders:

'You're l-l-lucky, you know. They say a birth-mark is a sign of l-l-luck.'

Nikolai gave him a radiant white-toothed grin, dived into the water and reappeared snorting.

'Come off it, mate!' he shouted. 'I've been an

---

*P. N. Wrangel (1878-1928), Whiteguard general, one of the leaders of the counter-revolution in South Russia (1918-1920). After the defeat of his forces by the Red Army he fled the country.—*Tr.*

orphan since I was a kid and sweated all my life as a labourer—some luck!'

And he swam away to the yellow sand-bar embracing the Don.

II

The cottage where Nikolai was billeted stood on a cliff overlooking the river. From the windows could be seen the green sweep of the far bank and the burnished steel of the water. On stormy nights the waves beat at the foot of the cliff, the shutters moaned and sobbed, and to Nikolai it seemed that the water was creeping up through the chinks in the floor and shaking the cottage as it rose.

He had often made up his mind to move to a different billet but had somehow never got round to doing so. And now it was autumn.

One frosty morning he went out on to the steps of the porch, shattering the fragile silence with the clatter of his iron-tipped boots, walked down into the little cherry orchard and stretched out on the grass, which was all grey and tearful from the dew. He could hear the mistress of the house in the cowshed, urging her cow to keep still, and the deep, demanding cries of the calf, and the stream of the milk ringing against the side of the pail.

The wicket gate creaked and the watch-dog began to bark.

'Commander at home?' came the voice of the platoon sergeant.

Nikolai raised himself on one elbow.

'Over here! What's the matter now?'

'Messenger from the village. Says a band has broken through from the Sal District and taken the Grushino State Farm.'

11

'Bring him to me.'

The messenger tried to lead his horse towards the stable. But the animal was bathed in hot sweat and in the middle of the yard it sank down on its forelegs, then rolled over on its side and gasped out its last breath, gazing with glassy eyes at the watch-dog, which by now was almost choking with fury. The horse had died because the dispatch the messenger had brought was marked with three crosses and he had galloped it forty versts without a rest.

Nikolai read the village chairman's request for aid and went into the front room, buckling on his sword and thinking to himself: 'Another band. And just as I was hoping to go and study somewhere... The Commissar's always on at me about it. You're a squadron commander, he says, and can't even spell properly. But was it my fault I never got through the parish school? Can't he see that?.. And now here's another band... More blood... I'm sick of living like this, I've had enough.'

As he went out on to the steps, loading his carbine, the thoughts were still racing through his head, like horses over a well-worn track: 'If only I could go to town... Just go and study...'

He strode towards the stable past the dead horse, glanced at the black ribbon of blood oozing from its dusty nostrils and turned away.

III

Mousy plantains curl over the hummocks and wind-licked ruts amid the bushy goose-foot and mallow. This track was once used for carting hay to the threshing barns that are dotted over the steppe like congealed splashes of amber; the main highway follows the hill, where the telegraph poles are. The poles march away into the whitish autumn murk, striding across gullies and ravines, and along with them, along the damp glistening track, an ataman leads his band—fifty Cossacks of the Don and the Kuban who have a grudge against Soviet rule. For three days, like wolves that have plundered a flock of sheep, they've been making their getaway by road and roadless steppe, and all this time Nikolai Koshevoi's detachment has been on their trail, watching out for them.

A hard-bitten lot they are, old army men, well seasoned, but all the same their ataman has to keep his wits about him. He stands up in his stirrups, scans the steppe with eyes that are like feeling hands, and counts the miles to the blue fringe of forest stretching away on the far side of the Don.

So he retreats, stealthy as a wolf, but Koshevoi's squadron is hard on his heels.

On fine summer days in the Donside steppes the wheat waves and rings like pure silver under the intense translucent sky. That's before the reaping, when the beard of the full-eared Garnovka wheat darkens like the fluff on the lip of a seventeen-year-old and the rye stretches up as though it would outgrow a man.

The bearded Cossack farmers sow their rye in strips on the loamy patches and sandy slopes and along the edges of the poplar groves. It never burgeons well; an acre won't yield more than six bushels, but they sow it because they can distil from it a spirit clearer than a maiden's tears, because this has been the custom for centuries, because their fathers and forefathers loved to drink, and because it was not for nothing that the Great Seal of the Don Cossack Army portrayed a drunken Cossack sitting stripped to the waist astride a barrel of wine. It's a wild and heady

brew that goes around the villages and stanitsas*
in autumn and sends the Cossacks' tall red-topped
hats swaying unsteadily along by the willow fences.

That's why the ataman himself is never sober;
that's why the gun-crews and drivers all loll tipsily
on their machine-gun carts.

It's seven years now since the ataman saw the
smoke of his home fires. First, a German prison
camp, then service with Wrangel, then Constantinople
melting in the sun, then internment behind barbed
wire, then a Turkish felucca with its tarry, salt-caked
lateen, then the rushes of the Kuban, and then—this
marauding band.

That's what the ataman's life has been, if he
cares to look back. His heart has hardened as the
imprint of an ox's cloven hoof hardens by a steppeland pool in the heat of summer. A mysterious,
hidden pain gnaws at his vitals, sickens every muscle,
and he feels that this sickness can be neither forgotten
nor drowned in drink. Yet still he drinks—never a
day sober; for sweet and fragrant grows the rye in the
Donside steppe with its black greedy belly upturned
to the sun, and the brown-cheeked village women
whose husbands are away make a brew so pure there's
no telling it from spring water.

IV

The first frost came at dawn. It silvered the broad
leaves of the water-lilies and at day-break Lukich
noticed frail mica-coloured icicles on the wheel of
his mill.

Lukich had been feeling rotten ever since morning;

*Stanitsa—Cossack term for district centre and the dis-
trict surrounding it.—Tr.

14

there were pains in the small of his back and the dull ache made his legs so iron-heavy that they seemed stuck to the ground. He shuffled about the mill, every movement an effort, as though his flesh had in some strange way become detached from the bones. A brood of mice scurried out from under the millet scourer. He stared bleary-eyed at one of the rafters, where a pigeon was cooing briskly. With nostrils that looked as if they had been moulded out of steppeland loam the old man breathed in the musty odour of river slime and the smell of milled rye, listened to the unpleasant choking sound of the water sucking and licking at the piles, and tugged thoughtfully at his matted beard.

In the garden where he kept his bees Lukich lay down to have a rest. He went to sleep under his big sheepskin with his mouth hanging open and the warm sticky spit trickling on to his beard. Dusk daubed its shadows over the little cottage and the mill was soon enmeshed in milky shreds of mist...

When he awoke, two horsemen were riding towards him out of the forest. One of them shouted to him as he shuffled across the bee-garden.

'Come here, Granfer!'

Lukich gave him a suspicious look and stopped. In these troubled years he had seen more than enough of these armed men who took flour and fodder without asking, and for all of them he had a hearty dislike.

'Get a move on, you old goat.'

Lukich stepped out from between the hand-wrought hives, silently munching his faded lips, and halted at some distance from the strangers, eyeing them warily.

'We're Reds, Grandad. You needn't be afraid of us,' the ataman declared peaceably. 'We've been chasing a band and got left behind by the others.

15

Mebbe you've seen our detachment passing here-abouts?'

'Somebody went by.'

'Where did they go, Grandad?'

'Plagued if I know.'

'Any of 'em stay behind at the mill?'

'No one here,' Lukich replied curtly and turned his back.

'Just a minute, old man.' The ataman heaved himself out of the saddle, swayed drunkenly on his bow legs and with a strong whiff of home-brew on his breath said: 'We're liquidating Communists, Grandpa... Mark that! As for who we are, that's none of your business!' He stumbled and dropped the rein. 'It'll be your job to supply enough grain for seventy horses and keep quiet... And quick about it! Understand? Where's your grain?'

'Nothing here,' Lukich said, looking away.

'What's in that barn?'

'Just rubbish, I reckon... I've got no grain.'

'Very well, then. Come along!'

The ataman seized the old man by his collar, propelled him with his knee towards the crooked, sunken barn and flung open the door. The bins were full of wheat and barley.

'Isn't that grain, you old scoundrel?'

'Yes, son, it's grain... It's the left-overs. I've been saving it up all the year. And you want to feed it to horses...'

'So our horses can starve, for all you care, eh? Who're you for—the Reds? Asking for a bullet, are you?'

'Oh, have mercy on me, son! What have I done wrong?' Lukich pulled off his old cap, dropped to his knees and seized the ataman's hairy hands, trying to kiss them.

'Speak! Do you love the Reds?'

16

'Forgive me, gentle master! Pardon my foolish words. Have mercy, don't kill me,' the old man quavered, grovelling at the ataman's feet.

'Swear that you're not for the Reds... No, don't cross yourself! Eat dirt!'

The old man scooped up a handful of dirt and munched it with his toothless gums, moistening it with his tears.

'All right, now I believe you. Get up, old one!'

And the ataman laughed as he watched the old man's helpless efforts to rise on his stiff legs. The other horsemen rode up and ransacked the bins of barley and wheat, scattering what was left under their horses' hooves and carpeting the yard with golden grain.

V

Daybreak was grey and misty, wrapped in a murky wetness.

Lukich slipped past the sentry, and not by the road but by a path that he alone knew struck out for the village dozing wearily in expectation of the dawn.

He hobbled as far as the village windmill and was about to cross the cattle track into a side-lane, when the vague shapes of horsemen loomed up in front of him.

'Who's there?' the challenge rang out urgently in the stillness.

'It's me,' Lukich mumbled, and began to tremble.

'Who is it? Where's your pass? What are you hanging around here for?'

'I'm the miller... From the watermill over there. I've got business in the village.'

'What business? Now then, off you go to see the commander! Forward march!' one of the horsemen shouted, riding at Lukich.

17

The old man felt the horse's warm lips on his neck and limped along as fast as he could into the village.

They halted on the square, outside a small tiled cottage. His escort heaved himself grunting out of the saddle, tethered his horse to the fence and clumped up the steps with his sabre rattling at his side.

'Follow me!'

There was a light showing in the windows. They entered.

The tobacco smoke made Lukich sneeze. Pulling off his cap, he made a hurried sign of the cross towards the front corner of the room.

'We've just picked up this old feller on his way to the village.'

Nikolai lifted his tousled head from the table and asked sleepily but sternly: 'Where were you going?'

Lukich stepped forward with a joyful gasp.

'Why, it's you, son! Our own folk. And I thought it was them devils again... I was so darn frightened I was afraid to ask. I'm the miller. You stopped at my mill when you were passing through Mitrokha's Wood. I gave you some milk to drink, laddie. Don't you remember?'

'Well, what have you got to tell us?'

'This is what I want to tell you, lad. After dark yesterday that gang of bandits, they stopped at my mill and took all the grain for their horses. They wanted to kill me. Their head man, he says, "Swear you're one of us!" and he made me eat dirt.'

'Where are they now?'

'They're still there. They've got vodka with 'em and they're guzzling it in my front room, the unclean devils. So I ran over here to report to you, Your Honour. Mebbe you'll be able to deal with them.'

'Tell the boys to saddle up!' Nikolai rose from the bench with a smile at the old man and reached wearily for his greatcoat.

VI

The dawn came.

Nikolai, grey-cheeked from so many sleepless nights, galloped up to the machine-gun cart.

'As soon as we attack, let 'em have it on the right flank. We've got to smash their wing.'

He rode back to the squadron, which was drawn up in open order.

Beyond a clump of stunted oaks a column of horsemen appeared, riding along the highway four abreast with their machine-gun carts in the middle.

'Charge!' Nikolai yelled, and as a rumble of hooves rose behind him lashed his stallion into a gallop.

The machine-gun on the edge of the wood broke into a mad chatter and smartly, as if at exercises the riders on the highway swung into formation for the counter-charge.

A wolf sprang out of the thickets on the hillside, its coat bristling with burrs. It listened for a moment, with its head thrust forward. Shots were crackling not far away and the roar of shouting came in a long surging wave.

Crack! A shot sounded in the alder thickets and from somewhere on the other side on the hill the echo muttered back across the ploughed land: *crack!*

And again more shots. *Crack! Crack! Crack!* And back across the hill. *Crack! Crack! Crack!*

The wolf stood there for a while, then loped unhurriedly into the yellow clump of unmown rushes in the gully.

'Hold out! Don't leave the machine-guns! Into the wood! Into the wood, curse your mothers' blood!' the ataman bellowed, rising in his stirrups.

But the drivers and gunners were already hacking

19

at the traces, and the bandits' line, raked by constant machine-gun fire, was breaking into uncontrollable flight.

The ataman turned his horse and saw a lone rider flying towards him, sabre whirling, cloak spread out like wings. By the field-glasses dangling from his chest and the fine black cloak the ataman guessed that this was no ordinary Red Army man galloping towards him, and he reined in his horse. From a distance he made out the young, beardless face, convulsed with fury, the eyes narrowed in the wind. The ataman's horse danced and reared under him as he tugged at the pistol caught in his sash and shouted:

'Come on, you hairless puppy! Brandish your sabre!... I'll brandish you!'

He fired into the black cloak as it loomed up before him. The horse galloped another twenty yards and fell, but Nikolai threw off his cloak and ran towards the ataman, firing as he went. Nearer and nearer...

Beyond the trees someone screamed like an animal and broke off. The sun went behind a cloud and shadows glided over the steppe, the highway, and the woods that the winds and autumn had laid bare.

'He's just a stripling, a hot-headed puppy, and death shall have him for it!' the ataman muttered to himself. He waited until the lad's magazine was empty, then loosed the reins and swooped like a hawk.

Leaning out of his saddle, he swung his sabre and felt the sudden weakening of the body as it collapsed under the blow and slumped obediently to the ground. The ataman dismounted, ripped the field-glasses off the dead man, glanced at the legs, still quivering in agony, looked round and squatted down to take off his victim's chrome-leather boots. With his foot grinding into the dead man's knee he deftly slipped off one of the boots. But on the other leg the sock seemed to have rucked up and the second boot would not come off. With an angry curse he tugged again and pulled off boot and sock together. Just above the ankle he saw a mole as big as a pigeon's egg. Slowly, as though afraid to waken the lad, he turned the cold face towards him, soaking his hands in the blood that foamed from the mouth. He stared hard for a moment, then seized the angular shoulders in an awkward embrace.

'Son!' he said dully. 'My Nikolai! My own flesh and blood!'

His face darkening, he shouted:

'Speak! Just one word! How? Why?'

He fell forward, peering into the dying eyes; he lifted the blood-stained lids and shook the limp, unresisting body... But Nikolai had his teeth firmly clenched on the bluish tip of his tongue, as though afraid he might unwittingly speak of something immeasurably great and important.

The ataman clasped his son's cold hands to his breast and kissed them, then gripped the barrel of his pistol between his teeth and, as the cold steel grew clammy with his breath, fired straight into his own mouth.

In the evening, when riders appeared beyond the trees and the wind brought the sound of voices, of neighing horses and jingling stirrup-irons, a carrion kite rose reluctantly from the ataman's shaggy head, soared up and melted into the grey, autumnally faded sky.

1924

THE HERDSMAN*

I

From the east, from the grey-brown, sun-scorched steppe, from the white, cracked salt-marshes a hot wind has been blowing for sixteen days.

The earth is charred, the grass withered and yellow; the wells clustered along the high road are dry in every vein; and the ears of corn, still wrapped in leaf, are wilted and drooping, like bent-backed old men.

At noon a bell splashes its brassy clangour over the dozing village.

It is hot, and very still, but for the sound of feet shuffling along by the fences and stirring up the dust, and the tapping of the old men's sticks on the bumps in the road as they grope their way along.

The bell calls them to a village meeting. The subject to be discussed is the hiring of a herdsman.

The Executive Committee's office is abuzz with talk and thick with tobacco smoke.

The chairman taps on the table with a stump of pencil.

'Citizens! Our old herdsman says he's not going to mind the herd any longer; the pay's not good enough, he says. So we, the Executive Committee, propose Frolov, Grigory, in his place. He's one of us, born and

*English translation ©Progress Publishers 1975.

22

bred. He's an orphan, and a Young Communist... His father, as you know, was a cobbler. Just now he's living with his sister and they've nothing to live on. So, I reckon, citizens, you'll show consideration and take him on to look after the herd.'

This was too much for old man Nesterov and he at once began to squirm and fidget on his rheumaticky hindquarters.

'He won't do for us! It's a big herd and what kind of herdsman will he make! They'll have to be minded on the far pasture because there's no grazing here-abouts, and he's not used to the job. We'll find half the calves missing by autumn.'

Ignat the miller, a sly old fellow, spoke up with honeyed malice in his nasal little voice.

'We can find a herdsman without the Executive. That's our business. What we need is an old man who's reliable and has a way with animals.'

'Quite right, Grandad!'

'If you hire an old man, citizens, you'll only be more likely to lose your calves. Times are different now; there's a mighty lot of thieving about every-where.' This was the chairman speaking, firmly and kind of expectantly; and suddenly he was supported by somebody at the back of the room.

'No, an old man won't do. They're not cows, ye' know, they're all yearling calves. You need to be able to run like a dog to keep up with 'em. If that herd bolts, your old man will lose all his innards afore he rounds 'em up!'

Laughter rocked the room, but the old miller kept his end up in a half whisper from the back.

'This is nothing to do with the Communists... It ought to be decided with prayers, not just anyhow.' And the old nuisance stroked his bald pate.

But to this the chairman reacted with fitting sternness.

23

'Now then, citizen, none of this heckling... I'll have you turned out of the meeting for that kind of talk.'

So, at daybreak, when the smoke was rolling out of the chimneys like wads of greasy cotton wool and streaming low over the square, Grigory rounded up the herd of a hundred and fifty head of cattle and drove it through the village and over the grey bleak hill beyond.

The steppe was pimpled with greyish marmot burrows and the little animals were uttering their long anxious cries; now and then a bustard rose out of the stunted grass in the ravines, its silvery feathers gleaming.

The herd was quiet and the patter of the calves' cloven hooves on the dry wrinkled ground was like steady rain.

Grigory had his sister Dunyatka with him, as herdsman's mate. Her flushed freckled cheeks were laughing, so were her lips and eyes. In fact, she was laughing all over, for she had seen only seventeen springs, and when you are seventeen everything— your brother's gloomy face, the calves with their floppy little ears, snipping off the weeds as they trot along, and even the fact that you haven't had a crust of bread to eat today or yesterday—seems just a huge joke.

But Grigory was not laughing. Grigory's forehead under his shabby cap was steep and furrowed and his eyes were tired, as though he had lived much longer than his nineteen years.

The herd loped along calmly, spread out along the sides of the road like speckled swathes of grass. Grigory whistled up the laggards and turned to his sister.

'By autumn, Dunya, we'll have earned enough grain to go to town. I'll get into the Workers' Faculty there and fix you up—something educational, too, maybe. We'll have all the books we want in town,

24

Dunya, and the folk there eat proper bread, not stuff with grass in it like ours.'

'But where shall we get the money to go there with?'

'Oh, don't be daft! They'll pay us twenty poods of grain, and there's the money for you. We'll sell it at a ruble a pood. And we'll have millet and dung-fuel to sell too.'

Grigory halted in the middle of the road and started drawing figures in the dust with his whipstock and totting them up.

'But what are we going to eat now, Grisha? We've got no bread at all.'

'I've still got a bit of dry bun in my bag.'

'If we eat that, what shall we have tomorrow?'

'Someone will come out from the village tomorrow and bring us flour. The chairman promised...'

The noonday sun scorched down. Grigory's sackcloth shirt grew damp with sweat and stuck to his shoulder-blades.

The herd plodded on restlessly. The gadflies were stinging the calves and the sultry air was alive with the lowing of cattle and the buzz of flies.

By evening, just before sunset they reached the pen. Not far away was a pond and a shelter with its straw thatch nearly rotted away by rain.

Grigory broke into a run and, rounding the herd, pounded heavily up to the pen and pulled open the wattle gate. One by one he let them in through the black square entrance, counting them as they entered.

II

They built a new shelter on a mound that bulged like a huge pea on the far side of the pond. Together they plastered the walls with dung, and then Grigory

25

thatched the roof with brushwood.

The next day the chairman came out on horseback. He brought with him half a pood of maize flour and a bag of millet.

In the cool of the shelter he squatted down on his haunches and lit a cigarette.

'You're a good lad, Grigory. You'll do your spell of minding the herd and in autumn we'll go to the district centre. Mebbe from there you'll manage to go on somewhere to study. There's a feller I know at the public education department who'll give you a helping hand...'

Grigory's face crimsoned with joy and, when he saw the chairman off, he held his stirrup for him and squeezed his hand warmly. And for a long time he stood watching the curly wisps of dust streaming from under the horse's hooves.

The withered steppe, always unhealthily flushed at sunrise and sunset, choked in the heat at noon. As Grigory lay on his back gazing at the hill wrapped in a melting blue haze, it seemed to him that the steppe was alive, and that it must be suffering under its measureless burden of villages, stanitsas and towns. The soil seemed to heave and pant for breath and somewhere deep down, under thick layers of rock, there must be surging and throbbing another life that was altogether different and beyond his ken.

Even in broad daylight he was awed by the thought.

His eyes tried to count the countless folds in the steppe; he stared at the quivering haze and at the herd dotted over the brown grass and told himself that he was cut off from the world like a slice of bread cut from a loaf.

One Saturday evening Grigory drove the herd into the pen as usual. Dunyatka had lit a fire by the shelter and was boiling up a porridge of millet and sorrel leaves.

Grigory sat down by the fire and poked the pungent-smelling dung bricks with his whipstock.

'Grishaka's calf has gone sick. We ought to send word to its master.'

'Should I go to the village?' Dunyatka said, trying to sound as if she didn't care.

'No, you shouldn't. I won't be able to mind this lot alone.'

He smiled. 'Feeling lonely, eh?'

'Yes, I am that, Grisha dear. We've been living in the steppe a whole month and only seen one person in all that time. If we're out here all summer, I'll forget how to speak.'

'Stick it, Dunya. We'll be going to town in autumn. We'll both go to school and, when we've got through, we'll come back here and farm the land according to science. There's nothing but ignorance around here and folk are all sound asleep. None of 'em can read or write and there's no books.'

'But no one will take us on. We're just as ignorant as all the rest.'

'Yes, they will. When I was in the stanitsa I read a book by Lenin that the group secretary had. It says the proletariat must govern, and about education it says the poor folk ought to be educated.'

Grigory straightened up and the bronze glow of the sunset played on his cheeks.

'We've got to study, so as to be able to govern our republic. In the towns the workers hold power, but the chairman of the stanitsa Soviet is a kulak; and in the villages too, most of the chairmen are from the well-to-do.'

'I could scrub floors and take in washing to earn money while you did your studying.'

The dried dung smoked and smouldered and occasionally burst into spluttering flame. The steppe was silent, half asleep.

III

A militiaman on his way to the district centre brought word from Politov, the secretary of the Party group, that Grigory was to come and see him in the stanitsa.

Grigory set out before dawn and by midday was looking down from a hill at the bell-tower and the little houses round it, roofed with sheet-iron or straw.

Footsore, he plodded on to the square.

The club was in the priest's house. He walked over the fresh straw matting into a large room.

The shutters were closed and the room was in semi-darkness. By the window, Politov was busy planing some wood to make a frame.

'Yes, I've heard all about it, lad,' he said with a smile, offering Grigory a perspiring hand. 'Well, never mind I've made inquiries at the district centre. They wanted some lads for the oil mill there, but they've got a dozen more than they need already. You'll have to mind the herd till autumn, then we'll send you away to study.'

'I'll be glad to keep the job I've got. Those kulaks in our village were dead against having me as herdsman. He's one of them Young Communists, they says, he's a godless heathen. He won't pray while he minds the herd...' And Grigory gave a weary laugh.

Politov swept the shavings away with his sleeve and sat down on the window-sill, watching Grigory from under his damp, matted eyebrows.

'You're as thin as a rake, Grigory. How are you off for grub out there?'

'I get enough.'

For a time neither of them spoke.

'Well, let's go over to my place. I'll give you some fresh literature. We've just had a batch of books and newspapers from the district centre.'

They walked down a street that led to the grave-yard. Hens were cleaning their feathers in the ash-heaps. Somewhere a well-sweep was creaking and the oppressive stillness rang in the ears.

'Why don't you stay on for a bit? We're going to have a meeting. The boys have been asking about you. Where's Grisha, they say, what's he up to these days? You'll be able to see them all again. And I'll be giving a talk on the international situation. Why don't you stay the night with me and go back to-morrow?'

'I can't stay the night. Dunyatka won't manage alone. I'll stay for the meeting and go off at night, as soon as it's over.'

It was cool in Politov's porch. The sweet fragrance of dried apples was mingled with the stench of horse sweat from the collars and traces hanging on the walls.

In the corner stood a barrel of kvass; beside it, a sagging bed.

'This is my little nook. I find it too hot in the house.'

Politov bent down and with great care drew out from under the unbleached linen sheet some back numbers of *Pravda* and two books.

He pushed them into Grigory's hands, then picked up a small well-patched sack and shook the mouth open.

'Hold that.'

Even while Grigory held the top of the sack, his eyes kept straying to the printed sheets.

Politov poured handfuls of flour into the sack until it was half full, shook it down, and then slipped away into the front room of the cottage.

He reappeared carrying two slabs of bacon fat, which he wrapped in a rusty-looking cabbage leaf and also put into the sack.

'Take that with you when you go back,' he said gruffly.

Grigory flushed. 'But I can't take all that...'

'Yes, you can.'

'I won't.'

'What the hell!' Politov shouted, turning pale and staring fiercely at Grigory. 'And you call yourself a comrade! Starve to death, would you, without telling anyone! Take it, or you're no friend of mine.'

'I don't like to take the last you have.'

'The last, my foot!' Politov said, more gently now, as he watched Grigory huffily tying up the sack.

The meeting ended just before dawn.

Grigory set out across the steppe. The sack of flour was tugging at his shoulders, and his blistered feet were burning, but he strode on with cheerful fortitude into the blazing dawn.

IV

At daybreak, when Dunyatka crept out of the shelter to gather dry dung for fuel and saw Grigory coming across from the cattle pen at a run, she guessed something was amiss.

'Is something wrong?'

'Chrishaka's calf has died... And another three have taken ill.' Grigory heaved a deep breath. 'Go to the village, Dunya, and tell Grishaka and the others to come out here. Their calves are sick, tell 'em.'

Dunyatka tied her kerchief in a hurry and set off across the hill with the sun creeping over the mound behind her.

When he had seen his sister off, he walked slowly back to the pen.

The herd had strayed down into the hollow, leaving the three sick calves lying by the fence. By midday they were dead.

From then on Grigory spent his time rushing from the herd to the pen. Two more animals fell sick.

One dropped down on the damp mud by the pond and looked up at Grigory, uttering long mournful cries, its bulging eyes glazed with tears; and the salty tears flowed down Grigory's bronzed cheeks, too.

At sunset Dunyatka arrived with the owners.

Old granfer Artem poked his motionless calf with his stick and said: 'Ay, that's plague, that is. The whole herd will go down with it now.'

They flayed the beasts and buried the carcasses not far from the pond, topping the grave with a fresh mound of dry black earth.

The next day Dunyatka took the road once again; seven calves had all fallen ill at once.

The days followed one another in grim procession. The pen grew empty. And Grigory felt his heart growing empty with it. Out of one hundred and fifty head of cattle there were only fifty left. The owners came out in their carts, flayed the dead animals, dug shallow pits in the hollow, threw earth over the bloody carcasses and drove away. It was becoming hard to get the herd to enter the pen; the calves lowed in fright, scenting the blood and the death that was creeping invisibly among them.

At dawn, when the wan-faced Grigory opened the creaking gate of the pen and let the herd out to pasture, it always had to cross the still damp soil of fresh graves.

And all day long there was the stench of decaying flesh, the dust kicked up by the bolting animals, the incessant helpless lowing, and the sun, hot as ever, following its leisurely course across the steppe.

Hunters came out from the village and fired their guns along the fences to scare the dread disease away from the pen. But the calves went on dying and the herd grew smaller every day.

Grigory began to notice that some of the graves had been disturbed, and not far away he discovered gnawed bones; the herd had often been restless at night and now it grew timid. The stillness would suddenly be broken by a wild lowing and the herd would charge about the pen, smashing down the fences. When they broke out of the pen, they would come over to Grigory's shelter in bunches and sleep by the fire, breathing heavily and chewing the cud.

Grigory did not guess what was wrong until one night, when he was awakened by barking. Dragging on his coat, he rushed out of the shelter and found himself surrounded by calves and felt the rub of their dewy flanks as they nuzzled up to him.

He stood for a while at the entrance to the shelter, then whistled his dogs, and from a ravine near by, known as Snake Gully, was answered by the high-pitched howling of wolves. From the thorn bushes girdling the hill came yet another answering howl.

He went back into the shelter and lighted the oil lamp.

'Dunya, d'ye hear that?'

The howling died away with the stars, at dawn.

V

Ignat the miller and Mikhei Nesterov came out that morning. Grigory was in the shelter mending his shoes. The old men entered. Ignat took off his cap and, screwing up his eyes against the slanting sunrays that fell across the earthen floor of the shelter, raised his hand to make the sign of the cross before the small photograph of Lenin pinned up in the corner. Only just in time did he see what it was, retrieved his hand and put it hastily behind his back, spitting fiercely.

'So... You have no sacred icon, eh?'

'No.'

'Who's that in the sacred corner?'

'Lenin.'

'Well, that's the reason for all our trouble! Where God is not, there is sickness. That's why all our calves have died. Oh, Almighty Lord, our merciful...'

'The calves died, Grandad, because no one called in the vet.'

'We got on all right without this vet of yours before. You're getting too learned. You should cross your sinful forehead a little more often, then no vet would be needed.'

Mikhei Nesterov rolled his eyes and bellowed: 'Take down that godless heathen from the place of honour! It's because of you, you rotten blasphemer, that all the cattle have died off.'

Grigory's face paled slightly.

'Give orders in your own house. Don't yell at me. That's the leader of the proletariat—'

Mikhei ruffed up like a cockerel and went purple in the face.

'If you're in our service, you'll serve our way!' he shouted. 'We know your kind. You'd better look out, or we'll soon settle your hash.'

And they clamped on their hats and went out without another word.

Dunyatka stared at her brother in fright.

The next day Tikhon the smith came out from the village to see how his calf was faring.

He squatted by the shelter, smoking, and talked with a wry and bitter smile on his face.

'It's a rotten life we lead. They've got rid of the old chairman, and Mikhei Nesterov's son-in-law is in charge now. They do everything to suit themselves. Yesterday there was a share-out of land. But as soon as any of the poor get a good strip, there has to be a

33

fresh share-out. We'll have the wealthy riding on our backs again before long... They've grabbed all the good land, Grigory boy. There's only sandy stuff left for us. That's the way things are nowadays.'

Until midnight Grigory sat by the fire, writing clumsily with a bit of charred wood on broad saffron-coloured maize leaves. He wrote about the unfair dividing-up of the land and about the attempt to scare away the cattle plague with guns instead of calling in the vet, and then he gave the bunch of dry scrawled maize-leaves to Tikhon.

'If you're ever at the district centre,' he said, 'ask where the newspaper *Krasnaya Pravda* is printed. And give 'em this. I've written it as clear as I can, but don't fold the leaves or you'll rub the charcoal off.'

The smith took the leaves carefully between his scarred, coal-blackened fingertips and pushed them down his shirt-front, next to his heart. Before he left he said with a smile:

'I'll walk to the district centre. Mebbe I'll find Soviet rule there... I can do a hundred and fifty versts in three days. I'll look you up in about a week's time, when I get back.'

VI

Autumn brought rain and a gloomy dankness.

Dunyatka went off early one morning to fetch food from the village.

The calves were grazing beyond the hill. Grigory had his sheepskin over his shoulders and was thoughtfully crushing a faded roadside thistle between his palms as he followed the herd. Just before the brief autumn twilight fell, two horsemen rode over the hill.

With clumping hooves they cantered up to Grigory. Grigory recognized one of them as the new chairman,

34

Mikhei Nesterov's son-in-law; the other was the son of Ignat the miller.

The horses were in a lather.

'Hullo there, herdsman!'

'Hullo.'

'We've come to see you.'

Shifting his weight in the saddle, the chairman fumbled to unbutton his greatcoat with numbed fingers. Having done so, he pulled out a yellow sheet of newspaper and let it flap open in the wind.

'Did you write this?'

Before Grigory's eyes danced the words he had written on those leaves of maize about the sharing out of the land and the cattle losses.

'Come along with us.'

'Where?'

'Over there, into the ravine... We want to talk to you...' The chairman's blue lips were twitching and his eyes were shifty and threatening.

Grigory smiled.

'Say it here.'

'I can say it here if you like—'

He whipped a revolver out of his pocket and, reining in his bucking horse, snarled, 'Write to the papers, would you, you dirty swine?'

'But why...'

'I'll tell you why—I'm to be had up in court because of you! Tell tales, would you?—Speak up, you commie bastard!'

And without waiting for an answer he fired straight at Grigory's silent mouth.

Grigory fell under the hooves of the rearing horse, gasped once, dug up a tuft of damp brownish grass with his clawing fingers, and was still.

Ignat's son jumped off his horse, scooped up a clot of black earth and stuffed it into Grigory's mouth as the blood came foaming forth.

35

The steppe is broad and no man has measured it. It has many roads and tracks. The autumn night is dark as pitch and hoof marks will be washed clean away by rain...

VII

Drizzle. Dusk. The road across the steppe.

But it's not hard going for someone who has a bag on his back with only a loaf of barley bread in it, and a good stick in his hand.

Dunyatka is striding along the side of that road. The gusty wind is tearing at the hem of her ragged jacket and pushing her on from behind.

All around lies the sombre, desolate steppe. It is growing dark.

The mound comes into view not far from the road, and on it stands the shelter with its windblown roof of brushwood.

Dunyatka staggers like a drunk as she turns towards it, and at the settled grave she flings herself down flat on her face.

Night...

Dunyatka has reached the well-worn highway that leads straight to the railway station.

The going is easy, for in the bag on her back she has only a loaf of barley bread, a tattered book whose pages reek of the bitter steppeland dust, and her brother Grigory's sack-cloth shirt.

But when the grief swells up in her heart and the tears scorch her eyes, she finds a place that is out of sight, takes the rough unwashed shirt out of her bag, presses her face into it and feels the smell of her brother's sweat. And for a long time she lies very still...

The versts roll by. The wolves bay in the steppeland thickets, protesting at the wretched life they lead, but Dunyatka strides along at the side of the road. For she is going to town, where there is Soviet rule, where the proletarians are studying, so that in the future they will be able to govern their republic.

Lenin's book says it is so.

1925

THE GETLING*

Misha dreamed that Grandad was coming towards him, angrily swinging a long cherry switch he had cut in the orchard.

'Come along, come along, Mikhailo Fomich,' Grandad said sternly. 'You've got a good hiding due to you.'

'What for, Grandad?'

'For stealing all the eggs out of the tufted hen's nest to pay for the merry-go-round.'

'But Grandad,' Misha protested desperately, 'I never went near the merry-go-round all summer.'

But Grandad only smoothed his beard, and stamped his foot, and said, 'Come along, you scamp. And let your pants down.'

Misha cried out in his sleep, and that woke him. His heart was thumping as if he'd really had a taste of the switch. He opened one eye, just wide enough to peep around him. It was already light. Outside the window spread the warm blow of dawn. Out in the entrance voices sounded. Misha lifted his head. He could hear his mother's voice, shrill, excited, and half choked with laughter. And Grandad kept coughing. There was someone else there, too, someone with a booming voice.

*English translation ©Progress Publishers 1975.

Misha rubbed the sleep out of his eyes. The outside door opened and shut. Grandad came trotting into the room, his spectacles bobbing up and down. For a minute Misha thought the priest must have come, with the choristers, because Grandad had fussed around just that way when they'd come at Easter. But it wasn't the priest that came pushing into the room behind Grandad. It was a stranger, a great big soldier in a black greatcoat and a ribboned cap with no peak. And Mother with her arms around his neck, squealing with excitement.

The man shook Mother off, and yelled out, 'Where's my offspring?'

Misha was scared, and hid under the blanket.

'Minyushka,' Mother called, 'wake up, sonny. Here's your Daddy, back from the wars.'

And before Misha knew it the soldier had pulled him out of bed and thrown him up as high as the ceiling, and caught him again, and pressed him close, poking that prickly red moustache of his at Misha's lips, and cheeks, and eyes. It was wet, too, that moustache, and it tasted of salt. Misha tried to wriggle free, but that didn't work.

'What a fine big Bolshevik I've got me,' Daddy roared. 'The boy will soon outgrow his Dad! Ha! Ha!'

He couldn't stop playing with Misha. One minute he'd sit the boy on his palm and twirl him like a baby, and the next throw him up again as high as the ceiling beams.

Misha stood it as long as he could. But finally he made a stern face, pulling his eyebrows together the way Grandad did, and grabbed his father's moustache in both hands.

'Put me down, Daddy.'

'Oh, no, I won't.'

'Put me down. I'm no baby, for you to play around with.'

Daddy sat down, and set Misha on his knee.

'How old are you, then, big boy?' he asked, smiling.

'Getting on for eight,' Misha answered sullenly.

'Well, don't you remember those steamboats I made for you, the year before last? And how we sailed them in the pond?'

'I remember,' Misha cried, and his arms went timidly up around his father's neck.

And that was when the fun began. With Misha riding pickaback on his shoulders. Daddy pranced round and round the room, kicking out suddenly and neighing, just like a real horse. Misha could hardly catch his breath, it was all so exciting. Only Mother kept pulling at his sleeve.

'Misha!' she cried. 'Go and play in the yard. Clear out, I tell you, you young rascal.'

She pestered Daddy, too.

'Put the boy down, Foma. Do put him down. Let me have my fill of you, my own dear love! Two whole years we've been apart, and you spend your time playing with the child!'

Daddy set Misha down.

'Run and play with the boys awhile,' he said, 'and later on I'll show you what I've brought you.'

Misha's first impulse, as he shut the door behind him, was to stay right there in the entrance and listen in on what the grown-ups were talking about. But then it occurred to him that not one of the village youngsters knew his Dad was back. And off he went, across the yard and straight through the kitchen garden, trampling through the potato plants, and down to the pond.

He splashed about awhile in the evil-smelling, stagnant water, then rolled in the sand until he was coated with it, and took a last dip in the pond. Hopping first on one foot, then on the other, he got into his trousers. As he was thinking of starting for

40

home, Vitya came along—the priest's youngster.

'Don't go, Misha. Let's have a dip, and then come to my place to play. Mother says you can come.'

With his left hand, Misha hoisted his trousers up and adjusted the only remaining strap of his braces over his shoulder.

'I don't want to play with you,' he said. 'Your ears stink.'

'That's the itch,' Vitya said, pulling his knitted shirt off over his skinny shoulders. And maliciously screwing up one eye, he went on, 'And you're no Cossack. Your mother got you in the gutter.'

'A lot you know about it!'

'I heard our cook telling my mother.'

Misha's bare toes dug into the sand.

'Your mother's a liar,' he declared, looking down at Vitya from his superior height. 'And anyway, my Daddy fought in the war, and your Dad's a blood-sucker, gobbling other people's bread.'

'And you're a getling', the priest's boy retorted, on the verge of tears.

Misha stooped and picked up a big smooth pebble. But the priest's boy, controlling his tears, gave him a sugary smile.

'Don't get mad, now, Misha,' he said. 'There's no sense in fighting. I'll give you my dagger, if you want it, the one I made out of a piece of iron.'

Misha's eyes gleamed, and he threw away his pebble. But then he remembered Daddy and retorted scornfully.

'My Daddy brought one home from the wars. It's far better than yours.'

'You're making it up,' Vitya drawled, unconvinced.

'Making it up yourself! If I say he did, that means he did. And a good gun, too.'

'Umph! Rich, ain't you!' Vitya snorted, with a wry, envious grin.

'And he's got a cap with ribbons on it, and gold letters on the ribbon like in those books of yours.'

It took Vitya some minutes to think up an answer to that. His forehead went all wrinkly, and he scratched absently at the white skin of his belly.

'My Daddy is going to be a bishop, one of these days,' he said finally. 'And your Dad's nothing but a herdsman. There!'

But Misha was tired of standing there, arguing. He turned away and made for home.

'Misha! Misha!' the priest's boy called after him. 'I've got something to tell you.'

'Go on then.'

'Come nearer.'

Misha came nearer, his eyes screwed up suspiciously, 'Well, what is it?'

Dancing around in the sand on his skinny bow-legs, the priest's boy cried, with a gloating smile,

'Your Dad's a Commie. And the minute you die, and your soul flies up to heaven, God will say to you, "Your Dad was a Communist, so you must go straight down to Hell." And down there, the devils will roast you in their frying-pans.'

'Well, and they'll roast you too.'

'My Daddy's a priest. Ah, you're just an ignorant fool. What's the sense of talking to you?'

That frightened Misha. Silently, he turned and ran for home.

By the fence he looked back and shook his fist at the priest's boy.

'I'm going to ask my Grandad. If you've been telling lies, you'd better keep away from our yard.'

He climbed the fence and ran for the house. He could just imagine that frying-pan, with him, Misha, frying in it. Scorching hot, and the sour cream bubbling and foaming all around him. A shiver went down his back. He must find Grandad, quick, and ask him all about it.

Just then he saw the sow. It had got its head stuck through the wicket gate and all the rest of it was outside. It was pushing with all its might, waggling its little tail and squealing desperately. Misha flew to the rescue. But when he tried to open the gate, the sow began to wheeze.

So he climbed on its back, and then, with a final effort, the animal tore the gate off its hinges and made off across the yard as fast as it could go. Misha dug his heels into its sides, and it carried him along so fast that his hair streamed in the wind. By the threshing floor he jumped off. And when he looked around, there was Grandad, on the house porch, beckoning.

'Come here, young man!'

It never occurred to Misha what Grandad was after. The vision of the frying-pan filled his mind again, and he ran straight to the porch.

'Grandad, Grandad, do they have devils in Heaven?'

'I'll show you where they have devils. Just you wait. A proper whipping—that's what you want, you little scamp! What do you mean, riding horseback on the sow?'

Grandad grabbed Misha by the forelock, so he couldn't make off, and called into the house to Mother, 'Come, have a look at this smart son you've reared.'

And out came Mother.

'What's he been up to now?'

'Why, what's he been up to but riding around the yard astride the sow, raising the dust behind him!'

'The sow that's due to litter?'

Mother's hands flew up in horror.

Before Misha could so much as say a word in self-defence, Grandad had undone his belt and, holding up his trousers with one hand, pushed Misha's head between his knees with the other. He gave Misha a thorough strapping, to the stern refrain of, 'Don't ride that sow again. Don't ride that sow.'

Misha began to bawl, but Grandad quickly put a stop to that.

'Is that how you love your father, you young brat? Here he's just come home, all tired out, and trying to sleep, and you raise such a howl!'

So Misha had to keep quiet. He aimed a kick at Grandad, but couldn't reach far enough. Then Mother grabbed him and pushed him indoors.

'Sit still, child of a hundred devils! If I take my hand to you, I won't be as soft as Grandad.'

Grandad sat on the kitchen bench, glancing now and again at Misha who stood with his face to the wall.

Misha swung around rubbing away one last tear with his fist.

'Just you wait, Grandad,' he said, his back pressed to the door.

'Threatening your Grandad, are you?'

Grandad started to undo his belt again. Misha pushed against the door until it swung a little open.

'Threatening me, are you?' Grandad repeated.

Misha disappeared outside the door. But he peeped in again, on the alert for Grandad's slightest movement, and shouted,

'Just you wait, Grandad. When all your teeth are gone don't ask me to chew for you, because I won't.'

Grandad came out on the porch just in time to see Misha's head and his blue trousers flash in shaggy hemp in the garden. The old man shook his stick menacingly, but his lips, in the shelter of his beard, were smiling.

* * *

Father called him Minka. Mother called him Min-yushka. Grandad, when peacefully inclined, called him a scamp; but at other times, when Grandad's

44

bushy grey eyebrows drew together in a frown, it would be, 'Come here, Mikhailo Fomich. Your ears want pulling.'

Everyone else—gossipy neighbours, children, the whole village—called him Mishka when they didn't call him the Getling.

Mother had borne him out of wedlock. True, she had married his father, herdsman Foma, only a month later. But the bitter nickname, the Getling, stuck to Misha for life.

Misha was a smallish child. His hair, in early spring the colour of sunflower petals, had been bleached by the June sun into a rough, streaky mop. His cheeks were freckled like a sparrow's egg, and his nose was always peeling from exposure to the sun and frequent dips in the pond. He had only one good point, this bow-legged little Misha: his eyes, blue and mischievous, peeping out of their narrow slits like bits of half-thawed river ice.

It was for those eyes that Misha's father loved him, yes, and for his active, restless temperament. From the wars, Dad had brought his son home a honey cake, stone-hard with age, and a pair of slightly worn top-boots. Mother wrapped the boots in a towel and put them away in the chest, and as for the cake, Misha pounded it with a hammer, that very evening, and ate it to the very last crumb.

Next morning Misha woke at sunrise. He scooped a bit of tepid water from the pot, smeared his grimy face with it, and ran out of doors to dry.

Mother was in the yard, busy with the cow. Grandad, who was sitting by the house, beckoned to Misha.

'Dive under the barn, little scamp. I heard a hen clucking in there. It must have laid an egg.'

Oh, Misha was always ready to oblige his Grandad. He crawled under the barn, crawled out on the other

45

side, and off he ran, kicking up his heels, through the kitchen garden—glancing back now and then to see if Grandad was watching. By the time he got to the fence, his legs were all in a rash from nettles. Grandad waited and waited, until he lost patience and crawled under the barn himself. He got smeared with chicken droppings, and half blind in the damp darkness, bumped his head painfully against all the floor beams before he got through to the other side.

'Aren't you stupid, Misha, searching all this time for one little egg! As if a hen would lay anything out there! Right by this stone, that egg ought to be. Misha! Where are you, anyway?'

Grandad got no answer. Brushing the dirt from his trousers, he crept out from under the barn and peered towards the pond. Sure enough, Misha was there. He shrugged and turned away.

By the pond, the village youngsters were crowding around Misha.

'Where was your Dad?' someone asked. 'At the wars?'

'That's right.'

'Doing what?'

'Fighting—what else?'

'Come off it. All he fought was lice. And the rest of the time he sat by the kitchen door, gnawing bones.'

The youngsters screamed with laughter, hopping up and down and pointing at Misha. Tears of bitter resentment filled Misha's eyes. And to top it all, Vitya, the priest's boy, had a dig at him.

'Your Dad's a Communist, ain't he?'

'I don't know.'

'Well, I know. He's a Communist. He sold his soul to the Devil, that's what my Daddy told me this morning. Yes, and pretty soon all the Communists are going to be strung up.'

46

A hush fell over the youngsters. Fear clutched at Misha's heart. His Dad strung up? For what crime? Through clenched teeth, he retorted,

'My Dad's got a great big gun, and he'll kill off all the bourjoos.'

'Oh, no, he won't,' Vitya declared triumphantly. 'My Daddy won't give him the holy blessing, and if he has no blessing he can't do anything at all.'

Proshka, the shopkeeper's son, jabbed Misha in the chest.

'Don't you talk too big about that Dad of yours,' he cried, his nostrils twitching. 'He grabbed all my Dad's goods when the Revolution came. And my Dad, he says, "Just you wait till the tables turn. First thing I do, I'll kill that herdsman Foma." '

And Natasha, Proshka's sister, stamped her foot and yelled,

'Beat him up! What are you waiting for, boys?'

'Beat the Communist brat!' someone else cried.

'That Getling!'

'Give it to him, Proshka!'

Proshka swung a switch, and struck Misha across the shoulder. The priest's boy, Vitya, hooked Misha's leg and brought him down heavily, flat on his back in the sand.

Yelling, the boys threw themselves upon him. Natasha, squealing shrilly, tore at his neck with her sharp nails. Someone kicked him painfully in the belly.

Misha shook Proshka off, struggled to his feet, and made for home, zigzagging like a hunted hare. Loud whistles followed him, and someone threw a stone, but no one gave chase.

Only in the prickly green shelter of the hemp in the kitchen garden did Misha stop for breath. He sank down on the damp, fragrant soil, and wiped the blood away where his neck had been scratched. And then he began to cry. The sunlight, working its way down through the dense leafage, tried its best to peep into his eyes. It dried the tears on his cheeks, and tenderly kissed the curly, reddish crown of his head, as Mother sometimes did.

Misha sat among the hemp for a long time—until the tears stopped flowing. Then he got up and went slowly into the yard.

His father was there, in the shed, tarring the wagon wheels. His cap had slipped to the back of his head, and its ribbons hung free. He was wearing a blue-and-white striped shirt. Misha sidled up to the wagon and stood silently watching. After a while, when he had summoned up the courage, he touched Daddy's hand, and asked, in a whisper,

'What did you do at the war, Dad?'

'Why, I fought, son,' Daddy returned, smiling under his red moustache.

'The boys... The boys say all you fought was lice.'

Again Misha choked with tears. But Daddy only laughed and swept Misha up in his arms.

'They're lying, son. I was on board a ship. A big ship, that sailed the seven seas. And then I fought in the wars.'

'Who did you fight?'

'I fought the bosses, Sonny. You see, you're still too small, so I had to go to the wars and fight for you. Why, there's a song they sing about it.'

His father smiled again, and, tapping out the time with his foot, sang softly:

> *Oh, my little Minka, Misha mine,*
> *Don't you go to the wars. Let your Daddy go.*
> *Daddy's old. He's lived his life.*
> *And you're still too young to take a wife!*

Misha forgot all about his troubles, and laughed aloud—laughed at the way his Dad's red moustache

48

bristled just like those plants Mother made brooms out of, and the way his lips smacked under the moustache, opening and shutting the round black hole of his mouth.

'Run along now, Minka,' Daddy said. 'I have to put the wagon to rights. In the evening, when you go to bed, I'll tell you all about the war.'

* * *

The day dragged like a lonely road across the endless steppe. At long last, the sun went down. The herd swept through the village. The dust clouds settled, and the first star peeped out shyly from the darkened sky.

Misha got awfully tired of waiting. Mother took so much time milking, and then straining the milk! And then she went down into the cellar and fooled around there for what must have been an hour! Misha hung around her, squirming with impatience.

'Mother! Ain't it supper-time yet?'

'Hungry? You'll just have to wait.'

But Misha gave her no peace. He followed her everywhere ... down to the cellar, and up again to the kitchen—clinging like a leech, hanging to her skirts.

'Mo-o-other! Su-upper!'

'Get out of my way, you little nuisance. If you're so hungry, you can take a hunk of bread.'

There was no quieting him. Even the slap his mother finally gave him did no good.

When supper came, he gobbled his food down hastily and dashed away to the other room. He flung his trousers behind the chest and dived straight into bed, under Mother's bright patchwork quilt. He lay very still, waiting for Daddy to come and tell him about the wars.

49

Grandad knelt before the icons, whispering prayers, bowing right down to the floor. Misha lifted his head to watch. Resting on hand, Grandad bent forward painfully until his forehead bumped on the floor boards. And just at that moment Misha banged his elbow against the wall.

Again Grandad whispered his prayers awhile, and then bowed his head to the floor—bump! And again Misha banged his elbow against the wall—bang! Grandad got angry.

'I'll teach you, you imp, the Lord forgive me! Bang the wall again, and I'll bang you!'

There would surely have been trouble, only just then Daddy came into the room.

'What are you doing here, Minka?' Daddy asked.

'I always sleep with Mother.'

Daddy sat down on the edge of the bed. He didn't say anything for a while, just sat there twisting his moustache. Finally, he suggested, 'I thought you'd sleep with Grandad, in the kitchen.'

'I don't want to sleep with Grandad.'

'Why?'

'Because of his moustache—it just stinks of tobacco.'

Daddy sighed, and twisted his own moustache again.

'All the same, Sonny, you'd better sleep with Grandad.'

Misha pulled the blanket up over his head, then peeped out again to mumble sulkily,

'You slept in my place yesterday, and now you want it again. Go and sleep with Grandad yourself.'

Sitting up suddenly, he pulled Daddy's head down and whispered in his ear,

'You'd better go and sleep with Grandad, because Mother won't want to sleep with you anyway. You stink of tobacco too.'

'All right, then, I'll go and sleep with Grandad. Only then I won't tell you about the wars.'

Daddy got up and headed for the kitchen.

'Daddy!'

'Well?'

'Sleep here, if you want to,' Misha said resignedly, getting out of bed. 'Now will you tell me about the wars?'

'Yes, now I will.'

Grandad got into bed first, leaving room for Misha on the outside. And after a while Daddy came into the kitchen, moved a bench up to the bed, and sat down. He had lit one of his evil-smelling cigarettes.

'Well, then, it was this way... Do you remember when the field next to our threshing floor belonged to the shopkeeper?'

Yes, Misha remembered that—remembered how he had liked to run up and down between the rows of tall, fragrant wheat. He had only to climb the stone fence of the threshing floor, and there he was, right in the wheat. It was taller than he was, and hid him entirely. The heavy, black-bearded ears tickled his cheeks, and there was a smell of dust, and daisies, and the steppe wind.

'Misha,' Mother would call after him, 'don't go too far in the wheat. You'll lose your way.'

'Well,' Daddy went on after a while, gently stroking Misha's hair, 'and do you remember the time we rode out past Sandy Hill, you and me, to the field where our wheat grew?'

Misha remembered that too: the narrow, crooked little strip beside the road, out past Sandy Hill, and the day he'd been there with Daddy and they'd found the wheat all trampled by somebody's cattle. Headless stalks, swaying in the wind; and scattered, broken ears on the ground, mixed with the dirt. Daddy's face had twisted terribly, and a few tears

51

had rolled down his dust-grimed cheeks—Daddy's cheeks. Misha's big, strong Daddy! And that had made Misha cry, too.

On the way home, Daddy had asked Fedot, the watchman at the melon patch,

'Who spoiled my field?'

And Fedot had spat and answered,

'The shopkeeper went past, driving some cattle to market, and he drove them through your field. On purpose.'

Daddy drew his bench up closer.

'The shopkeeper and the other big-bellies, they grabbed all the land, and there was no place left for the poor people to grow their grain. And that's how things were everywhere—not only here in our village. Oh, but they were hard on us, in those days. We'd nothing to live on. So I got a job herding the village cattle. And then I was drafted to the army. Things were bad in the army, too. The officers would beat us for the least little thing. Well, and then the Bolsheviks came along, and they had a leader by the name of Lenin. Not a big man to look at, but real learned, for all that he comes of peasant stock—just like you and me. And those Bolsheviks, they said such things, all we could do was stand and gape. "What are you thinking of, workers and peasants?" they would say. "Take a broom to all the lords and officials, and drive them out for good. Everything belongs to you."

'That was the way they talked to us, and we couldn't say a thing. Because, when we thought it over, we saw they were right. So we took the land and the estates away from the masters. Only the masters, they didn't like it. They couldn't be happy without their land. And they got mad, and went to war against us—against the workers and the peasants. So you see, sonny, how it was.

'And that same Lenin, the Bolsheviks' leader, he

roused the people up the way you turn up the soil with a plough. He roused the workers and the soldiers, and didn't they go for those masters! And didn't the feathers fly! The soldiers and the workers got to be called the Red Guard. And I was in the Red Guard too. We lived in a huge big house, the Smolny it was called. You should see the great long halls there, sonny, and the rooms—so many rooms, you could get lost yourself there.

'I was on sentry duty one day, by the front door. It was bitter cold, and all I had to keep me warm was my army coat. The wind seemed to blow right through me. And then two men came out of the door. And as they passed, I saw that one of them was Lenin. And he came right up to me and asked, in such a friendly way,

' "Aren't you cold, Comrade?"

'And I said to him,

' "No, Comrade Lenin, the cold can't beat us, nor no enemy neither. Once we've got the power in our own hands, we'll never give it back to those bourgeoises."

'He laughed, and shook my hand warmly, and then he went on towards the gate.'

His father fell silent. He got out his tobacco pouch and a bit of paper, and rolled himself a new cigarette. When he struck a match to light it Misha saw, on his bristly red moustache, a glittering teardrop—like the drops of dew you can see of a morning, hanging from the nettle leaves.

'That's the sort he is. Everyone matters to him. He worries over every soldier, with all his heart. I saw him often after that day. He'd be going by, and recognize me from afar, and he'd smile and say, "So the bourgeois won't beat us, eh?"

' "Not they, Comrade Lenin," I'd say to him.

'And things turned out just as he said, Sonny.

We seized the land and the factories, and threw out the big-bellies, the bloodsuckers. Don't you forget, when you grow up, that your Dad was a sailor and fought four long years for the Commune. I'll die, some day, and Lenin will die too, but the things we fought for will live forever. Will you fight for the Soviets too, when you grow up, like your Daddy?'

'I will,' Misha cried, and sprang up in bed to throw his arms around Daddy's neck. Only he forgot about Grandad, lying there beside him, and thrust his foot against the old man's belly.

Grandad let out an awful grunt, and tried to catch Misha by his forelock. But Daddy took Misha in his arms and carried him into the other room.

After a while, still in Daddy's arms, Misha fell asleep. But first he thought deeply about that extraordinary man, Lenin, and about the Bolsheviks, and the wars, and the great ships. Half dozing, he heard low voices, and breathed the sweetish smell of sweat and tobacco. And then his eyes shut tight, and wouldn't open any more—as if someone had pressed a hand over them.

Hardly was he asleep, when a city rose before him. The streets were wide, with chickens wallowing in scattered ash-heaps everywhere you turned. There were ever so many chickens at home in the village, but in the city there were ever so many more. And the houses—they were just as Dad had said. You'd see a great big house, roofed with fresh reeds—and on its chimney another house, and on that one's chimney another still. And the top chimney of all reached right up to the sky.

And as Misha walked along the street, his head tilted back to see better, who should come striding up to him but a great, tall man in a red shirt.

'Why do you hang around doing nothing, Misha?' the man asked, in such a friendly way.

'Grandad said I could go out and play,' Misha answered.

'Well, and do you know who I am?'

'No, I don't.'

'I'm Comrade Lenin.'

Misha was so scared, his knees began to shake. He'd have made off, only the man in the red shirt took hold of his sleeve and said,

'You've got no conscience, Misha—not a scrap. You know perfectly well I'm fighting for the poor folk. Why don't you join my army?'

'My Grandad won't let me,' Misha explained.

'That's as you please,' Comrade Lenin said, 'only there's no getting things straight without you. You've just got to join my army, that's all there is to it.'

Misha took Comrade Lenin by the hand and said, most resolutely,

'All right then, I'll join your army without asking Grandad, and fight for the poor folk. Only if Grandad tries to whip me, you must stand up for me.'

'I certainly will,' Comrade Lenin said, and went off down the street. And Misha was so happy, he couldn't catch his breath. He wanted to shout, but his tongue went dry and stuck to the roof of his mouth.

Misha twitched suddenly in bed, bumped into Grandad—and woke.

Grandad's lips were moving, mumbling something through his sleep. Outside the window Misha could see the pale blue of the sky beyond the pond, and against it a pink foam of clouds floating across from the east.

* * *

Every evening, now, Daddy would tell Misha more tales about the wars, and about Lenin, and about all the different places he had seen.

55

Saturday evening the watchman from the village Soviet brought a stranger to the house—a squat little man in an army greatcoat, with a leather brief case under his arm.

'Here's a comrade Soviet official,' the watchman said to Grandad. 'Come from the town, he is, and he'll stay the night with you. Give him some supper, Grandad.'

'We can do that,' Grandad said. 'Only, Mister Comrade, what are your credentials?'

Amazed at Grandad's erudition, Misha paused, finger in mouth, to listen.

'All the credentials you want, Grandad,' the man with the leather brief case answered, smiling. And he turned to go into the house.

Grandad followed him, and Misha followed Grandad.

'What brings you to our village?' Grandad asked.

'I'm in charge of the new elections. You're to have new elections here, for the chairman and members of the village Soviet.'

After a while Daddy came in from the threshing floor. He shook hands with the stranger and told Mother to get supper ready.

After supper Daddy and the stranger sat down together on the kitchen bench and the stranger opened his leather brief case and got out a bunch of papers and showed them to Daddy. Misha hung around as close as he dared, trying to get a glimpse. Daddy took one of the papers and held it out to Misha.

'Look, Minka,' he said, 'this is Lenin.'

Misha seized the photograph—and, as he stared at it, his mouth fell open in surprise. The man in the photograph was not tall, and he had no red shirt on either—just an ordinary jacket. He had one hand in his trouser pocket, and the other flung forward, as though pointing out the way. Eagerly, Misha examined the photograph, indelibly printing on his memory the arched brows, the smile that lurked in the eyes and lips, every detail of the face.

The stranger reached for the photograph, locked it away in his brief case, and went to the other room to bed. He undressed and got into the bed, using his greatcoat as a blanket; but just as he was falling asleep the door suddenly creaked.

'Who's there?' he asked, lifting his head.

Bare feet came pattering across the floor.

'Who's there?' the stranger asked again. And then he saw that it was Misha, standing beside the bed.

'What is it, boy?' he asked.

For a moment Misha did not answer. Finally, summoning up his courage, he whispered,

'Look, Mister—give me your Lenin.'

The stranger did not say a word, just looked steadily down from his bed at Misha.

Misha was terribly frightened. Suppose the man was mean? Suppose he refused? Stumbling over the words in his eagerness, trying hard to stop his voice from trembling, Misha whispered,

'Give him to me, for keeps. I'll give you my tin box, a real good box, and every single knuckle-bone I've got, and'—with a desperate sweep of the arm—'yes, and the boots Daddy brought me, too!'

'But what do you want Lenin for?' the stranger asked, smiling.

He wouldn't agree, Misha thought. Bowing his head to hide the tears, he said heavily,

'I want him, that's all.'

The stranger laughed, pulled his brief case out from under the pillow, and gave Misha the photograph. Misha hid it under his shirt, pressing it tight against his heart, and raced back to the kitchen. Grandad woke up and grumbled,

'What's wrong with you, running around in the

middle of the night? I told you not to drink that milk at bedtime. If you've got to go that bad, you can piss in the slop pail. I'm not getting up to take you out of doors.'

Misha got into bed without answering. He lay very still, afraid to move for fear of crumpling the photograph, which he still held with both hands, pressed close to his heart. He fell asleep without changing his position.

It was scarcely light when he woke. Mother had just finished milking, and sent the cow off with the herd. At the sight of Misha she threw up her hands.

'What's bitten you? Why are you up so early?'

Holding the photograph tightly under his shirt, Misha slipped past his mother, across the threshing floor and under the barn.

Coarse burdock grew around the barn, and a thick, bristly green wall of nettles. Under the barn, Misha cleared a little space by brushing away the dust and sand. He wrapped the photograph in a big, yellowed burdock leaf, laid it in the cleared space, and weighted it down with a stone, so the wind could not blow it away.

It rained all day. Grey cloudbanks hid the sky. The yard was full of puddles, and swift rivulets raced one another down the street.

Misha had to stay indoors. But as evening fell Daddy and Grandad went off to the Soviet to attend the village meeting, and Misha, with Grandad's cap on his head, slipped out and followed them. The Soviet had its headquarters in the church lodge. Not without effort, Misha scrambled up the rickety, mud-caked porch steps. Inside, the place was packed. High up under the ceiling hung a cloud of tobacco smoke. At a table by the window sat the stranger, explaining something to the meeting.

Misha slipped stealthily to the back of the room

and sat down on the last bench.

'Comrades, those voting for Foma Korshunov as chairman of the Soviet please raise your hands.'

Prokhor Lisenkov, the shopkeeper's son-in-law, sitting right in front of Misha, shouted,

'Citizens! I object! He's no honest man. We found him out long ago, when he herded for the village.'

Then Fedot, the shoemaker, jumped up from his seat on the windowsill and shouted too, waving his arms excitedly,

'Comrades! The big-bellies don't want a herdsman for chairman. But herdsman Foma, he's one of the proletariat, he'll stand up for Soviet power.'

The wealthy Cossacks, bunched together by the door, began stamping and whistling. The room was filled with noise.

'Down with the herdsman!'

'Now he's back from the army, he can hire himself out again to be herdsman.'

'To hell with Foma Korshunov!'

Misha looked around for Daddy, and found him standing right near by. Daddy's face was white, and Misha turned white too, out of fear for him.

'Order, comrades,' the stranger yelled banging his fist down on the table. 'Or we'll throw out the rowdies!'

'Give us a real Cossack for chairman!'

'Down with Foma!'

'Down with him!..'

All the richer Cossacks were shouting now, and loudest of all the shopkeeper's son-in-law, Prokhor.

A huge, red-bearded Cossack with a ring in his ear climbed on a bench. His jacket was all patched and tattered.

'Brothers!' he cried. 'See what they're trying to do! The big-bellies, they want a man of their own for chairman. And then they can have things the way they were before...'

59

He shouted and shouted, the big Cossack with the ring in his ear, but through the din Misha could only make out a word or two here and there.

'The land... New share-out... Clay and sand for the poor folk, and the good black soil for themselves...'

'Prokhor for chairman!' the group at the door was yelling, 'Pro-kho-or! Kho-or! Kho-or!'

It was a long time before the din could be checked. The stranger shouted and shouted, frowning and spluttering. Cursing, most likely, Misha reflected.

When it got quieter, the stranger put the question loudly.

'Who votes for Foma Korshunov?'

A great many hands were raised, Misha raised his, too. Someone started counting, striding from bench to bench.

'Sixty-three ... sixty-four...' and, pointing to Misha's hand—'sixty-five.'

The stranger wrote something on a sheet of paper, and then shouted,

'Who votes for Prokhor Lisenkov?'

Up went the hands of twenty-seven of the richer Cossacks, and one more—miller Yegor's. Misha also raised his hand. But this time the man counting the votes, when he reached the back bench, happened to look down.

'Of all the little rascals!' he cried, grabbing Misha painfully by the ear. 'Get out of here, before I thrash you! Voting—and how do you like that?'

Laughter broke out. The man who had counted the votes dragged Misha to the door and pushed him out. Tumbling down the slippery porch steps, Misha recalled what Daddy had once said, arguing with Grandad.

'Who gave you the right?' he shouted.

'I'll show you who!'

Injustice is always a bitter thing!

When Misha got home he snivelled a bit, and complained to Mother. But she was cross, and said,

'Well, don't go where you're not wanted. Poking your nose in everywhere—you're a real trial to me!'

Next morning, while the family were still at breakfast, the sound of faraway music was heard. Daddy put down his spoon and said wiping his moustache,

'That's a military band.'

Misha was off like the wind. The door banged to behind him, and tap-tap-tap went his light footsteps across the yard.

Dad and Grandad went out too, and Mother leaned out of the window.

Rank upon rank of Red Army men were swinging up the village street like a surging greenish wave. The band marched in the lead, and the whole village rang to the blowing of its huge trumpets and the banging of its drum.

Misha was ready to burst with excitement. He spun around wildly on his heels, and ran to meet the marchers. A strange, sweet tingling filled his chest and rose to his throat. He looked up at the Red Army men's jolly, dust-grimed faces, at the musicians, with their cheeks puffed up so importantly. And he made up his mind, once and for all: he was going with them to fight in the war.

The dream he had had came back and, somehow mustering up the courage, he tugged at the cartridge pouch of one of the Red Army men.

'Where are you going? To fight in the war?'

'Where else? In the war, of course.'

'Who will you fight for?'

'For the Soviets, youngster. Here—get in the lines.'

He pulled Misha into the ranks. One of the men, grinning, flicked his finger against the boy's tousled head. Another fumbled in a pocket, got out a grimy

61

lump of sugar, and popped it into the boy's mouth. When they reached the square, the order was shouted down the lines,

'Halt!'

The Red Army men fell out, and threw themselves down to rest in the cool shade of the school-house fence. A tall, clean-shaven fellow with a sabre hanging from his belt, lounged up to Misha, twisting his lips in a smile.

'Where d'you come from?' he demanded.

Misha squared his shoulders importantly, and hitched up his trousers.

'I'm going to fight in the wars with you,' he declared.

'Comrade Battalion Commander!' one of the Red Army men called. 'Take him along to be your adjutant!'

Everyone roared with laughter. Misha was close to tears; but the man they called so strangely, 'battalion commander', frowned at the noise and answered sternly,

'What are you laughing at, blockheads? Of course we'll take him. Only on one condition.' Here he turned to Misha. 'Those pants of yours—they've only got one strap. We can't take you that way. You'd disgrace us. Look—I've got two straps to mine, and so have all the others. Just you run home as fast as you can, and get your mother to sew you on another strap. We'll be waiting for you here.' And, with a wink at the men resting in the shade of the fence, he shouted, 'Tereshchenko! Go and fetch a gun and an Army coat for our new Red Army man.'

One of the men got up and touched his hand to the peak of his cap.

'Right away,' he said.

And off he went, at the double.

'Double quick, now,' the battalion commander

said to Misha. 'Ask your mother to sew you on another strap, just as fast as she can.'

Misha looked up at him sternly.

'You won't go back on your word, will you?'

'Don't you worry.'

It was a long way home from the village square. By the time Misha reached the gate he was completely out of breath. He wriggled out of his trousers as he ran and tore barelegged into the house, crying,

'Mother! My pants! A strap!'

But the house was still and empty. A black swarm of flies hung, buzzing around the stove. Misha looked everywhere—the yard, the threshing floor, the kitchen garden—but there was nobody anywhere—neither Mother, nor Dad, nor Grandad. He ran back to the house. Looking around, he spied an empty sack. With a knife, he cut a long strip of sacking. He had no time to waste on sewing, and anyway, he had never learned to sew. He tied the strap hastily to the back of his trousers, threw it over his shoulder, and tied it to the front. That done, he flew out of the house and dived under the barn.

Still puffing for breath, he rolled the stone away, and glanced at the photograph. Lenin's outstretched hand pointed straight at Misha.

'There!' Misha whispered. 'Now I've joined your army.'

He wrapped the picture carefully in its burdock leaf, thrust it under his shirt, and rushed off down the street—holding the photograph safely in place with one hand, and hitching up his trousers with the other. Running past the neighbours' fence, he called,

'Anisimovna!'

'What's up? Anisimovna asked.

'Tell my folks not to wait dinner for me.'

'Where are you off to, little scamp?'

63

'To the wars!'—and Misha waved a hand in farewell.

But when Misha reached the square he stopped short, petrified. There was not a living soul in sight. The ground along the fence was littered with cigarette ends, and empty tins, and somebody's torn puttees. The band was playing again, away down at the end of the village, and you could hear the tramp of marching feet on the hard-packed dirt road.

One despairing cry, and Misha ran after them, just as fast as his legs would carry him. And he'd have surely caught them up, if it hadn't been for a big yellow dog sprawled right across the road by the tannery, its teeth bared in a snarl. By the time Misha had got round the dog, the music and the tramp of feet had died away.

* * *

A day or two later, a detachment of some forty men arrived at the village. These soldiers were not in uniform. They wore grease-stained work clothes, and shabby felt boots. When Daddy came home from the village Soviet for his dinner, he told Grandad,

'Get our wheat ready in the barn. There's a food detachment come, to collect the grain surplus.'

The soldiers went from house to house, testing the earthen floors of the sheds with their bayonets, digging up buried grain, and loading it on carts to be taken to the communal granary.

The chairman's turn also came. One of the soldiers, puffing at a tobacco pipe, asked Grandad, 'Well, Grandad, tell us the truth. How much grain have you buried?'

But Grandad only stroked his beard.

'My son is a Communist,' he answered proudly.

They went to the barn. The soldier with the pipe glanced at the bins, and smiled.

'Cart one binful to the granary,' he said, 'and keep the rest for yourself, for food and seed.'

Grandad hitched old Savraska to the cart. He sighed once or twice, and grumbled to himself, but he loaded the wheat—it filled eight sacks—and, with a helpless shrug, drove off to the granary. Mother wept a little, sorry to part with the wheat. Misha, after helping Grandad to fill the sacks, went over to the priest's, to play with Vitya.

The two boys settled down on the kitchen floor, with some horses they had cut out of paper. But just then the soldiers came—the same group that had been to Misha's home. The priest went scurrying out to meet them, stumbling over the hem of his cassock in his nervous haste, and invited them into the parlour. But the soldier with the pipe said sternly, 'It's your barn we want to see. Where do you keep your grain?'

The priest's wife came hurrying into the kitchen, her hair all in a mess.

'Would you believe it, gentlemen,' she said, with a foxy smile, 'we haven't any grain at all. My husband hasn't made his rounds of the parish yet.'

'Have you got a cellar anywhere?'

'No, no cellar. We've always kept our grain in the barn.'

Misha remembered very well how he and Vitya had played in a spacious cellar that they got into from the kitchen.

'What about the one under the kitchen where me and Vitya played?' he said, turning to face the priest's wife. 'You must have forgotten.'

The priest's wife laughed, but her face turned pale.

'You're imagining things, child,' she said. 'Vitya, why don't you two go and play in the orchard?'

The soldier with the pipe smiled at Misha, screwing up his eyes.

'How do you get to that cellar, youngster?' he asked.

'Don't you believe that silly child,' the priest's wife said, clenching her hands until the knuckles cracked. 'We have no cellar, gentlemen, I assure you.'

'Perhaps the comrades would like a bite to eat,' the priest suggested, smoothing the folds of his cassock. 'Just come into the parlour.'

Moving past the boys, the priest's wife pinched Misha painfully, but said, with the kindliest of smiles,

'Go out in the orchard, children. You're in the way.'

The soldiers exchanged glances and set about a careful examination of the kitchen, tapping the floor with the butts of their rifles. They shoved aside a table that stood by the wall, and lifted the sacking that lay under it. The soldier with the pipe pulled up one of the floor boards and looked down into the cellar.

'You ought to be ashamed,' he said, shaking his head. 'Telling us you have no grain, when your cellar's piled to the top with wheat.'

The priest's wife threw Misha such a look that he was frightened and wanted to get home just as fast as he could. He got up and made for the door. In the entrance the priest's wife caught up with him, seized him by the hair, and began shaking him. She was crying.

He jerked himself free and ran for home. Choking with tears, he told his mother what had happened. Her hands flew up in horror.

'What am I to do with you?' she cried. 'Get out of my sight before I thrash you!'

After that, when Misha's feelings were hurt, he would go straight under the barn, roll aside the stone, undo the burdock leaf, and, his tears rolling down on to the photograph, he would confide all his troubles to Lenin.

A week passed. Misha was very lonely. He had no one to play with. None of the youngsters round about would have anything to do with him. It was not only "getling" that they yelled after him now. There were new names the boys had picked up from their elders.

'Commie brat!' they would cry, and 'Commie bastard!'

Coming home from the pond late one afternoon, Misha heard his father's voice in the house, sounding very loud and stern. Mother was wailing as people do over the dead. Misha went inside. His father sat pulling on his boots. His army coat lay beside him already rolled.

'Where are you going to, Daddy?'

His father laughed.

'Quiet your mother, Sonny, if you can. She's breaking my heart with her crying. I have to go to the wars again, and she won't let me go.'

'Take me along with you, Daddy.'

Daddy pulled his belt tight, and put on his cap with the ribbons to it.

'Now, aren't you silly? How can we both go off together? You mustn't go till I get back. Or else who's to get the wheat in, when harvest comes? Mother has the house to tend to, and Grandad—he's getting old.'

Misha kept back his tears, and even managed to smile as he said good-bye to his father. Mother hung on Daddy's neck, as she had when he came home, and he had a hard time making her let go. Grandad sighed and, kissing Daddy good-bye, whispered in his ear.

'Look, Foma—what if you stayed home? Can't they get along without you? What will we do if you get killed?'

'Drop it, Dad. That's no good. Who's to fight for the Soviets, if the men all hide behind their women's skirts?'

'Ah well, go, then, if you're fighting for what's right.'

Turning away, Grandad furtively wiped away a tear.

They went as far as the village Soviet with Father, to see him off. A score or so of men were waiting there, all of them with rifles. His father took a rifle too. And then he kissed Misha good-bye again and marched away with the other men, down the road leading out of the village.

Misha walked home with Grandad. Mother dragged unsteadily behind. Here and there in the village dogs were barking. Here and there, a light showed in someone's window. The village had wrapped itself in the dark of night, as an old woman wraps herself in her black shawl. A light rain was falling, and somewhere out in the steppe lightning kept flashing, followed by the dull rumble of thunder.

They walked home in silence. But as they reached the gate Misha asked,

'Grandad, who's my Daddy gone to fight against?'

'Don't bother me.'

'Grandad!'

'Well?'

'Who's my Daddy going to fight?'

Bolting the gate, Grandad answered,

'There's some wicked men gathered together, right near the village. A band, people call them. Only to my mind they're just plain robbers. That's who your Dad's gone off to fight.'

'How many of them, Grandad?'

'Two hundred maybe—so people say. Off with you! It's high time you were in bed.'

In the night, Misha was wakened by the sound of

voices. He reached over to wake Grandad, but Grandad wasn't in the bed.

'Grandad! Where are you?'

'Shhh! Lie still and sleep.'

Misha got up and groped his way across the dark kitchen to the window. Grandad was there, sitting on the bench in nothing but his underclothes, his head poked out through the open window—listening. Misha listened too. Through the still night, he clearly heard the shooting, somewhere beyond the village. Scattered shots at first, and then regular volleys.

Bang! Bang-bang!

Like somebody hammering nails.

Misha was frightened. He moved up close to Grandad.

'Is that my Daddy shooting?' he asked.

Grandad did not answer. And Mother was crying again.

The shooting went on all night. At daybreak, all fell silent. Misha curled up on the bench and dropped into heavy, unrefreshing sleep. Soon a group of riders galloped down the street towards the village Soviet. Grandad woke Misha, and hurried out into the yard.

Smoke rose in a black pillar over the village Soviet. Flames licked at the nearby buildings and horsemen charged up and down the streets. One of them shouted to Grandad,

'Got a horse, old man?'

'Yes.'

'Hitch up, then, and go fetch your Communists. They're piled up in the brushwood. Tell their folks to bury them.'

Grandad quickly harnessed Savraska to the cart, took the reins with trembling hands, and drove off at a trot.

Shouts and screams rose over the village. The bandits were dragging hay from the lofts, and slaughtering sheep. One of them dismounted by Anisimovna's fence and ran into her house. Misha heard Anisimovna scream. The bandit came out, his sabre clattering in the doorway. He sat down on the porch, pulled off his boots, discarded his filthy foot-wrappings and replaced them with Anisimovna's bright Sunday shawl, torn roughly into two.

Misha climbed into Mother's bed and hid his head under the pillow. There he stayed until he heard the gate creak. Then he ran out of doors and saw Grandad, his beard all soaked with tears, leading the horse into the yard.

On the cart lay a man, barefoot, his arms flung wide. The man's head kept bumping against the back of the cart, and on the boards were great, dark pools of blood.

Swaying slightly, Misha went up to the cart and gazed into the man's face. It was criss-crossed with sabre cuts. The teeth were bared. One cheek had been sliced off, and hung by a shred of skin. A huge green fly sat on one bloodshot, goggling eye.

Misha was shivering with horror; but realisation did not come at once. He tried to turn away, and then his eyes fell on the blue-and-white striped sailor's shirt, all bespattered with blood. He started violently, as though someone had struck him, and turned again to stare wide-eyed at the dark, unmoving face.

'Daddy!' he cried, jumping up on to the cart. 'Daddy, get up! Daddy!'

He fell from the cart, and tried to run. But his legs buckled under him. On all fours, he crawled as far as the porch. And there he dropped, hiding his face in the sand.

*   *   *

Grandad's eyes had sunk deep, deep into their
sockets. His head was shaking, and his lips moved
soundlessly.

For a long time he sat stroking Misha's hair,
without a word. And then, with a glance at Mother,
prostrate on the bed, he whispered,

'Come, Grandson, let's get out of here.'

He took Misha by the hand and led him out on to
the porch. As they passed the open door of the other
room, Misha shuddered and dropped his eyes. There,
on the table, lay Daddy, so stern and still. The
bloodstains had been washed away, but Misha could
not forget that glassy, blood-shot eye, and the green
fly on it.

At the well, Grandad fumbled endlessly, undoing
the bucket rope. Then he led Savraska out of the
barn, brushed the foam from the horse's lips with his
sleeve, and slipped on the bridle. He stood listening a
moment. The village rang with shouts and laughter.
Two of the bandits rode by, their cigarette ends
glowing through the dusk. One of them said, 'Well,
we showed them what's what with their surplus.
They'll know better in the next world than to go
grabbing people's grain.'

When the hoofbeats had died away Grandad bent
down and whispered in Misha's ear. 'I'm too old. I
can't get up on the horse. I'll put you up, Grandson,
and you ride straight to Pronin village. I'll show you
the way. The soldiers are there, the ones that passed
through the village with the drums and the bugles
that time. Tell them to come quickly, because
the bandits are here. Will you remember what to
say?'

Misha nodded. And Grandad lifted him on to the
horse's back, and tied his legs to the saddle with the

71

rope from the bucket, so he wouldn't fall off, and led the horse across the threshing floor and past the pond, past the bandits' pickets, and out to the open steppe.

'See,' Grandad said, 'that gully cutting into the hill? Keep to the edge of the gully, and don't turn off anywhere. It will bring you straight to the farm. Well—good luck, my boy!'

Grandad kissed Misha, and slapped Savraska lightly on the haunch.

It was a clear and moonlit night. Savraska jogged along at an easy trot, snorting now and again. The weight of the rider bumping up and down in the saddle was so small that the horse often slackened its pace. Then Misha would give the reins a shake, or slap the horse's neck.

Out in the fields, where the ripening grain stood thick and green, the quails were calling cheerfully. A tinkle of spring water rose up from the gully. A cool breeze blew.

Misha felt frightened, all alone in the steppe. He threw his arms around Savraska's neck—a shivering human morsel, clinging to the warm flesh of the horse.

The track crawled uphill, then down a bit, then up again. Misha kept whispering to himself, afraid to look back, afraid even to think. He shut his eyes, and his ears were blocked by the stillness.

Suddenly Savraska tossed his head, snorted, and quickened his pace. Misha opened his eyes. Down below, at the foot of the hill, lights were faintly twinkling. Carried by the wind came the sound of dogs barking.

For a moment, Misha's chilled heart warmed with joy.

'Gee up!' he cried, banging his heels against the horse's sides.

The barking was nearer now, and up the slope the outlines of a windmill stood out faintly in the night.

'Who goes there?' came the call from the mill.

Misha silently urged Savraska on. Cocks were crowing.

'Halt! Who goes there? Stop, before I fire!'

That frightened Misha, and he tugged at the reins. But Savraska, sensing other horses near, neighed loudly and burst forward.

'Halt!'

Shots rang out from somewhere by the windmill. Misha's scream was drowned in the thudding of hooves. Savraska wheezed, reared, and fell heavily on his right side.

Pain shot through Misha's leg, pain so fearful, so utterly unbearable, that he could not even cry out. And Savraska's weight pressed down, heavier and heavier, on the aching leg.

The sound of hooves came nearer, nearer. Two riders appeared. With a clatter of sabres, they dismounted, and bent over Misha.

'God save us! Why, it's just a youngster!'

'Not killed?'

A hand was thrust under Misha's shirt, and warm, tobacco-laden breath brushed his face.

'Alive,' the first voice said, with evident relief. 'Looks like the horse hurt his leg.'

Half-fainting, Misha managed to whisper,

'There's bandits in the village. They killed my Daddy. And burnt down the Soviet. And Grandad says for you to come, as fast as you can.'

Then everything went dim, and rings of colour began to swirl before Misha's eyes.

Daddy went by, laughing, twisting his red moustache, and a big green fly balanced, swaying, on his eyeball. And there was Grandad, shaking his head

73

reproachfully. And Mother. And then a little man with a high forehead, his arm pointing straight at Misha.

'Comrade Lenin!..' Misha cried in a stifled voice and with a great effort raised his head, smiling and holding out his arms.

1925

GOLDEN STEPPE*

In Moscow, at the headquarters of Proletarian Culture in Vozdvizhenka Street, at a literary evening organised by the Moscow Association of Proletarian Writers one may quite unexpectedly learn that steppeland feather-grass (not just feather-grass but 'grey plumed feather-grass') has a special smell of its own. And one may also hear how Red Army men died in the Don and Kuban steppes, gasping out flowery phrases with their last breath.

Some writer who has never had a whiff of gun-smoke in his nostrils tells you a touching story about the Civil War and Red Army men, who, of course, are always 'brothers', and about the fragrant grey plumed feather-grass, and the overwhelmed audience—mostly sweet young girls from secondary school—generously reward the narrator with rapturous applause.

In actual fact, feather-grass is a rotten wispy-white grass. A harmful grass, without any smell at all. No one ever drives a flock of sheep through it because the awns get under their skin and fester and the sheep die of it. The trenches overgrown with plantains and goosefoot (you can see them along the

*English translation © Progress Publishers 1975.

cattle tracks leading out of any stanitsa), those silent witnesses of fighting that took place not so long ago, could tell us about the horribly simple deaths of those who died in them. But in these trenches, crumbled by time and weather, the local pigs wallow for most of the day, sometimes the well-fed geese waddling home from the fields sit down beside them, and at night, when a waning moon rides low over the steppe, the lads from the stanitsa take their girls out to the trenches that are deeper and a bit more cosy.

As they lie there they talk of this and that, a groping hand encounters a hard object lying in the grass that turns out to be an unexpended clip of ammunition. The mildewed cartridges are stuck together, the sharp-nosed bullets harbour an unspoken threat, but the two lovers never ask themselves why the occupant of this trench didn't fire those bullets, never think where he might have come from or whether he had a mother. Smoking his cigarette, the boy mentions that the other day Dunya got an award of alimony from Grisha, that Prokhor has again been caught making moonshine, that Vanyura guzzled his own calf and collected the insurance on it! Now I ask you after that how could feather-grass have any smell at all!

Grandad Zakhar and I are lying under a wild blackthorn bush on a hill above the Don that has gone bald in the sun. A brown kite is hovering under a scaly ridge of cloud. The thorn leaves, mottled with bird droppings, offer us no shade. My ears are ringing from the heat and a glance down at the curly, rippling expanse of the Don or the wrinkled water-melon rinds at my feet fills my mouth with a thick, sticky saliva and it's too much trouble to spit it out.

The sheep are huddled together in a hollow beside a half-dry pool. With wearily sagging hindquarters they swing their matted tails and sneeze violently in the dust. By the dam across the pool a burly young lamb has dug its hind legs into the ground and is sucking hard at a dirty yellow ewe. Now and then it butts its mother's udder; the creature moans and arches her back to give more milk and I fancy I can see a look of suffering in her eyes.

Grandad Zakhar stirs himself and sits up beside me. Pulling off his knitted woolen shirt, he peers at it with his weak eyes and starts feeling for something in the folds and seams. Grandad is only one year short of his three scores and ten. His bare back is ingeniously patterned with wrinkles and his shoulder blades jut out sharply under the skin, but his eyes are still blue and youthful and the glance from under his grizzled brows is quick and piercing.

With some difficulty he holds the louse he has caught between his shaky calloused fingers, holds it carefully and tenderly, then puts it on the ground as far away as he can, traces a small cross in the air with a thumb and two fingers and mutters huskily, 'All right, crawl away, varmint! You want to stay alive, don't ye? Ay, I thought so... Well, you've had a good suck, I must say, m'lady!'

Coughing and grunting, the old man pulls on his shirt and, throwing his head back, sips tepid water from his wooden flask. At every swallow his Adam's apple rises between the two limp folds hanging down from his chin to his throat; drops of water trickle over his beard and his lowered saffron lids redden in the glare of the sun.

Stoppering up the flask, he looks sideways at me and, catching my glance upon him, munches his lips dryly and stares away across the steppe. The far side of the hollow burns in a shimmering haze; the wind from the charred earth is fragrant with the honey scent of wild thyme. For a while the old man is silent, then pushes away his shepherd's crook and points past me with a tobacco-stained finger.

'See the tops of them poplars on t'other side of the gully? That's Topolevka, that is, used to be the Tomilins' estate. The village over there is called Topolevka, too. All the folk there used to be serfs. My father was one of 'em. He was coachman to Yevgraf Tomilin till the day he died. When I was only a little kid, he told me how his master bought him off a neighbour in exchange for a tame crane. And after my father died, I took over his job as coachman. The master himself was nearly sixty at the time. Great burly fellow he was, full-blooded too. He'd been in the Life Guards as a young man and, when he retired, he came to live the rest of his days on the Don. The Cossacks had taken over the family's land on the Don, but the government had given him another six thousand acres or more in the Saratov Province. Tomilin used to let it out to the Saratov folk while he himself lived in Topolevka.

'A queer man he was. He always went about in one of them long Georgian tunics made of the finest woollen cloth, with a dagger at the waist. When he decided to go visiting, we'd drive out of Topolevka and he'd give me the order, "Get 'em moving, damn you!"

'I'd use my whip and the horses would pull us faster than the wind could dry our eyes. Soon we'd come to a watercourse right across the road—the spring floods made plenty of 'em. You wouldn't hear the front wheels but there'd be a crack from the back—whang! We'd go on another half a mile, then "Turn round!" he shouts, and back we go at full speed to that watercourse... We'd be in and out of the damned thing about three times till we broke a spring or lost a wheel. Then my master, he'd climb out with a grunt and walk the rest of the way on foot, while I led the horses after him. And there was another game he had. We'd drive out of the grounds and he'd get up on the box beside me and snatch away my whip. "Liven up the leader!" he shouts. So I urge on the leader for all I'm worth, till the shaftbow is moving straight as a bullet, while he lashes the tracer with my whip. We had a team of three in those days and the tracers were Don thoroughbreds, like snakes, with their necks curving down as if they wanted to bite the ground.

'And he'd lash just one of them till the poor thing was all in a lather... Then he'd pull out his dagger, lean forward and slash the traces, as if he was cutting hair with a razor. Well, the horse would somersault about five yards and come down with a crash, blood pouring from its nostrils, and that was that! Then he'd do the same thing with the other tracer... And the leader goes on till it drops dead and even then my master wouldn't turn a hair, except that it would cheer him up a bit and get the blood working in his cheeks.

'He never went anywhere without something happening. Either he'd smash the carriage or kill the horses, then walk the rest of the way on foot... A cheerful feller my master was... Still, it's all over now, God be our judge... He used to make passes at my wife. She was a parlourmaid and she'd come running into the servants' quarters with her blouse all torn and crying her eyes out. And I'd see that her breasts were all scratched and bitten... Well, the master sent me off one evening to fetch the doctor. I knew there was no need and guessed what he was up to. So, I halted in the steppe, waited till it was dark and turned back. I drove into the estate by the back way, left the horses in the orchard, took my whip and went straight to our little room in the servants' quarters. I pulled the door open, not lighting any matches on purpose, and heard someone scuffling about on the bed... And as soon as my master got up, I let him have it with the whip, and that whip was tipped with lead... I spotted him trying to reach the window, so I gave him another one across the forehead. Then he jumped out of the window. I gave the wife a few strokes too, then went to bed. About five days later we made a journey to the stanitsa. While I was fastening the rug to the carriage, the master picked up my whip and started fingering the end. He fingered it for a bit, found the lead in the tip and asked, "Well, you dog, what have you put lead in your whip for?"

' "You told me to do it yourself," I answered.

'And he didn't say a word all the way to the first watercourse, just sat there whistling through his teeth. I had a quick look at him over my shoulder and noticed his hair was brushed over his forehead and his cap clamped hard down...

'About two years later he was paralysed. We took him to Ust-Medveditsa, called in the doctors and, when they came, he was lying on the floor, black in the face. All he could do was pull wads of banknotes out of his pocket and throw them at us: "Cure me, you swine!" he croaked. "I'll give you all I have!"

'But he died with his money, God rest his soul, and left his estate to his officer son. That young man, when he was a little boy, used to flay puppies alive, then make 'em run around the yard. He took after his father. But when he grew up, he gave up his pranks. He was very tall and thin, and always had dark circles under his eyes, like a woman... Used to wear gold specs on his nose, with a little cord to hold 'em. During the war against the Germans he'd been in charge of prisoners in Siberia, and after the revolution he turned up in our parts again. By that time my grandchildren had grown up and their father, my son, had died. I'd married off the older grandson, Semyon, but young Anikei was still single. I used to live with 'em, spending the rest of my days... In spring there was another revolution. Our folk drove the young master off his estate and the same day Semyon persuaded 'em to share out his land and take his property to their homes. And that's what they did. They all took their pick of the goods, parcelled out the land and started ploughing it. A week later the rumour went round that the master was coming back with a force of Cossacks to slaughter everyone. There was a village meeting and we sent two wagons to the station to fetch arms. During Holy Week we got our arms from the Red Guards and dug trenches outside Topolevka, right as far as the master's pond.

'See over there, where them rings of thyme are, beyond that gully, that's where the Topolevka folk manned the trenches. My grandsons were there with 'em, both Semyon and Anikei. The women brought 'em some food in the morning and, when the sun was at its height, over the hill came the cavalry. They spread out in attacking order with their sabres glinting blue. From our yard I saw the leader on a white horse wave his sword, then they rolled down that hillside like peas out of a sack. I spotted the master's white trotter by its gait, and that told me who the rider was... Well, our men beat 'em back twice, but the third time the Cossacks came up from behind and took 'em by surprise, and then the slaughter started... By sundown it was all over. I went out into the street and there was a bunch of our folk being driven to the estate by horsemen. So I took my stick and followed 'em.

'In the courtyard our Topolevka men were standing

81

herded together, just like them sheep over there. And all round them were Cossacks. So up I went. "Tell me, lads, where are my grandsons," I says.

'Both of them answered me from the middle of the bunch. Well, I had a word with 'em, then I saw the master come out on to the steps of the porch.

' "Is that you, Grandad Zakhar?" he bellows as soon as he sees me.

' "Yes, Your Honour!"

' "What are you doing here?"

'So I went up to the steps and knelt before him.

' "I've come to save my grandsons. Have mercy, master! I served your father, God bless his soul, all my life. Remember my zeal, master, and have pity on my old age!"

'And this was his answer: "Listen to me, Grandad Zakhar," he says. "I greatly appreciate your service to my father, but I can't pardon your grandsons. They're out-and-out rebels. Humble your soul, old man."

'I crawled up the steps and kissed his feet. "Have mercy, master! Remember, dear boy, how Grandad Zakhar tried to please you. Don't ruin me. My Semyon has a baby son at his mother's breast!"

'Well, then he lights one of them scented cigarettes, blows the smoke in the air, and says: "Go and tell the scoundrels to come to my quarters. If they beg forgiveness, well and good. I'll have 'em thrashed and enlist them in my detachment. Perhaps they will atone for their·shameful conduct by zealous service."

'So off I ran to the yard to tell my grandsons. Pulled at their sleeves I did. "Go and beg forgiveness, you madmen, don't get up from the ground till he pardons you!"

'But Semyon didn't as much as lift his head, just sat there on his haunches and scratched the ground with a stalk. And my Anikei, he took a long look at me, then snapped, "Go and tell your master that

Grandad Zakhar crawled on his knees all his life, and so did his son, but his grandsons don't want to any more. Tell him that!"

' "So you won't go, you son-of-a-bitch?"'

' "No, I won't!"'

' "It's all the same to you, you dirty scoundrel, whether you live or die, but why drag Semyon with you! Who'll look after his wife and child?"'

'I saw Semyon's hands begin to shake as he went on scratching with that stalk, not saying a word. Silent and stubborn as an ox, he was.

' "Go away, Grandpa. Don't soften our guts!" Anikei begged.

' "I won't go, curse your eyes! Semyon's Anisya will kill herself, if anything happens to him!"

'The stalk crunched in Semyon's hands and fell to the ground, broken.

'I waited. But still he didn't say anything.

' "Semyon, dear son, my only help! Come to your senses! Go to the master."

' "We've come to our senses and we won't go! You go and crawl!" Anikei blazed at me.

'And so I says to them: "You reproach me for kneeling before the master, do you? Well I'm an old man. Instead of my mother's breast I sucked the master's whip... And I'm not too proud to kneel before my own grandsons."

'So I went down on my knees, bowed my head to the ground and pleaded. The other men round them turned away, pretending not to see.

' "Go away, Grandad! Go away, or I'll kill you!" Anikei yelled. There was foam on his mouth and his eyes were wild like a roped wolf's.

'Then I turned away and went back to the master. I clutched his legs so tight he couldn't kick me away and held 'em till my arms went numb, but I could say nothing.

83

' "Where are your grandsons?" he asked.

' "They're afraid, master..."

' "Aha, so they're afraid..." And not another word. He kicked me with his boot right in the mouth and walked out on to the steps.'

Grandad Zakhar began to breathe very hard and fast; his face crumpled for a moment and turned pale; with a great effort he choked back the brief sobbing of an old man, wiped his dry lips with his hand and turned away. Beyond the pond the kite spread its wings obliquely, swooped into the grass and rose with a white-breasted bustard in its claws. The feathers scattered like ragged snowflakes and the brightness of them on the grass was unbearably harsh. Grandad Zakhar blew his nose, wiped his fingers on the hem of his knitted shirt, and went on with his tale.

'Well, I followed him out on to the steps, and there was Anisya running up with her baby. She pounced on her husband like that kite over there and just froze in his arms.

'The master called over the sergeant-major and pointed to Semyon and Anikei. The sergeant-major and six other Cossacks marched them into the master's poplar grove. I went after them, but Anisya left her child in the middle of the yard and tagged along behind the master. Semyon strode ahead of 'em all until he got to the stables, then sat down on the ground.

' "What are you at now?" the master asks.

' "My boot's pinching, I can't stick it any longer," says Semyon, and smiles.

'Then he took off his boots and gave 'em to me.

' "Wear them and good health to you, Grandpa," he says. "They've got good, double soles."

'So I took the boots and on we went. When we got to the fence, the Cossacks pushed 'em up against

84

it and started loading their guns, and the master stood by, clipping his nails with a little pair of scissors and I noticed how white his hand was.

' "Allow me, master," I says, "to take off their clothes. They've got good clothes, they'll be of use to us in our poverty. We'll wear them."

' "They can take them off."

'So Anikei pulled off his trousers, turned them inside out and hung them on one of the fence poles. Then he took the pouch out of his pocket, lit a fag, and stood with one leg forward, sending up smoke rings and spitting over the fence. And Semyon, he stripped himself naked, even took off his linen pants, but he forgot to take off his cap—I reckon he didn't know what he was doing... As for me, one moment I felt frozen, the next I was in a fever. I touched my forehead and the sweat on it was as cold as spring water... And there they stood side by side. Semyon's chest was all covered in thick hair and he just stood there, stark naked, with his cap on... Well, Anisya, being a woman, as soon as she saw her husband naked like that and with his hat on, she flung herself into his arms and twined herself round him like hops round an oak. Semyon pushed her away.

' "Get away, you hussy! Come to your senses! In front of others too! Can't you see how naked I am, curse you... Have you no shame?"

'But she'd let her hair down properly and kept shouting over and over, "Shoot us both."

'The master puts his little scissors in his pocket and asks, "Shall we shoot?"

' "Shoot, you rotten bastard!"

'And that was to the master!

' "Tie her to her husband!" he orders.

'Anisya realised what she had done and drew back, but it was too late. The Cossacks laughed and tied her to Semyon with a halter. Then the silly

85

woman fell down and pulled her husband down with her... The master came over to them and ground out through his teeth: "Perhaps for the sake of the child, you'll ask forgiveness?"

' "Yes, I will," Semyon groaned.

' "Very well, then, but you'll have to ask God because it's too late to ask me."

'And they shot them lying on the ground as they were... When they shot at Anikei he swayed on his feet, and didn't fall at once. First he sank to his knees, then twisted round suddenly and fell back face upwards. The master went over to him and asked very gently. "Do you want to live? If so, ask forgiveness. I'll let you off with fifty lashes and enlistment for the front."

'Anikei got a mouthful of gob, but he hadn't the strength to spit and it trickled down his chin. He turned white with anger, but it was no use—he had three bullets through him.

' "Lay him out on to the road!" the master ordered.

'So the Cossacks got hold of him and threw him over the fence, so that he fell across the road. And just then a company of Cossacks was riding out of Topolevka and they had two field-guns with them. So the master hops on to that fence like a cockerel and yells: "At the trot, driver, don't turn aside!"

'My hair just about stood on end. I was holding Semyon's clothes and boots, but my legs wouldn't hold me, they just gave way... Horses, y'know, they've got some sense in 'em and not one of 'em trod on my Anikei, they all stepped over him... I was clinging to the fence, I couldn't shut my eyes, and my mouth was all clogged up. The wheels of the gun went over Anikei's legs... First it was like crunching a crust of bread, then they were squashed flat as reeds... I thought Anikei would die of mortal pain, but he didn't even shout, just scooped earth off the road and crammed it in his mouth... Ay, chewed earth, he did, and looked up at the master without batting an eyelid, and his eyes were bright and clear as the sky...

'So that was that. Our master Tomilin shot thirty-two people that day. And the only one that came through alive was Anikei, thanks to his pride...'

Grandad Zakhar drank greedily from his flask, then wiped his faded lips and ended up reluctantly.

'Well, what's past is past. All that's left now are the trenches where our men fought to win some land for themselves. They're all overgrown with grass and weeds now... Anikei had to have his legs off. He's only got his arms to drag his body about with now. Still, he looks cheerful. Every day he and Semyon's little boy measure their height against the doorpost. The lad's outgrowing him... In winter sometimes he used to go out into the lane when they were driving the cattle down to the river to drink. He'd sit in the middle of the road with his hands up and the oxen would take fright and run on to the ice, nearly rupture themselves, they would, slipping and sliding. And he'd roar with laughter... Only once I noticed... In the spring it was. Our commune's tractor was going out to plough beyond the Cossack boundary, and he hitched himself on behind and went with it. I was grazing the sheep not far away and I saw my Anikei dragging himself along over the ploughed land. What's he going to do now, I wondered. Well, Anikei had a good look round to make sure there was no one near by, then he threw himself face downwards on the earth, and hugged one of the sods that had been turned up by the plough, fondling it and kissing it... He's in his twenty-fifth year and he'll never plough again. That's what makes him sad...'

The golden steppe was dozing in the smoky-blue

dusk; on the rings of fading thyme the bees were gathering their last honey for the day. The feather-grass, blond and brazen, was flaunting its crested plumes. The flock began to move down the hill towards Topolevka. Grandad Zakhar walked after it in silence, leaning on his crook. On the carefully embroidered coverlet of dust that was spread over the road there were two trails: one was a wolf-trail, the broad-padded tracks placed one upon another and far apart; the other, slicing the road with slanting stripes, was the trail of the Topolevka tractor.

Where the cart-track joined the forgotten weed-grown Hetman's Highway, the trails parted. The wolf-trail turned aside down the bluff, into impassable scrub and blackthorn, and on the road only one trail remained; it was regular and deeply imprinted and smelled of burnt paraffin.

1926

THE FOAL

Head foremost, legs outstretched, the foal emerged from its mother's body into a world of bright daylight, beside a dung-heap swarming with bottle-green flies. Its first experience in this world was terror. A shrapnel shell burst overhead, in a soft, swiftly melting grey-blue cloudlet, and the fierce whine of the explosion sent the damp, new-born thing cowering to its mother's feet. A stinking hail of shrapnel balls rattled down on the tiled roof of the stable. Some of the balls struck the ground, and the foal's mother—Trofim's chestnut mare—sprang to her feet, only to fall back again, with a brief moan, resting her sweat-streaked side against the protecting dung-heap.

In the oppressive silence that followed, the flies buzzed louder than ever. A cock, not bold enough to mount the fence and face the artillery fire, flapped its wings once or twice in the shelter of the burdocks and issued an unrestrained, if somewhat muffled, crow. In the house, a wounded machine-gunner was groaning querulously, breaking now and again into a hoarse scream or a string of furious curses. Bees hummed over the silky red poppies in the little front garden. In the meadow beyond the stanitsa a machine-gun was chattering and to the accompaniment of its brisk rat-tat-tat, the chestnut mare took advantage

89

of a pause between two shrapnel bursts and tenderly licked her firstling, who having found its mother's swollen udder, drank for the first time of the fullness of life, and of the infinite sweetness of a mother's love.

When the second shell burst beyond the threshing floor, Trofim came out of the house, slamming the door behind him, and headed for the stable. Rounding the dung-heap he flung up a hand to shade his eyes against the sun. And then he saw the foal, all atremble with the effort, sucking at the udder of his chestnut mare and, completely at a loss, he fumbled in his pockets for his tobacco pouch and with trembling fingers rolled a cigarette.

'So,' he said, when at last he managed to speak. 'So you've foaled, have you? You picked a nice time for it, I must say!'

His voice rang with bitter injury.

The mare looked indecently thin and weak. Blades of grass and bits of dung had stuck to her matted coat, but her eyes, though tired, shone with pride and joy, and to Trofim at least, her satiny upper lip seemed to crinkle into a smile. He led her to the stable, and when she began to eat, tossing her head and snorting into the nose-bag, he leaned against the door-post and inquired coldly, with a hostile glance at the foal, 'So this is what comes of having your fling, is it?'

The mare made no response.

'You might at least have got it from Ignat's stallion, instead of from God knows who. What do you expect me to do with a foal on my hands?'

Through the shadowed hush of the stable came the crunching of grain. A sunbeam filtered through a crack in the door, spilling gold on all it touched. Crossing Trofim's left cheek, it turned the red of his moustache and stubbly beard into gleaming copper, and deepened the dark furrows around his mouth. The foal stood there, on its long, thin legs, like a child's wooden toy.

'Kill it, shall I?'. Trofim demanded, pointing a crooked, tobacco-stained forefinger at the foal.

The mare rolled her bloodshot eyes, blinked, and threw a derisive look at her master.

*   *   *

That evening Trofim had a talk with his squadron commander.

'She got careful, that mare of mine. Wouldn't trot, wouldn't gallop. Always short of wind. So I gave her a look-over, and sure enough, she was in foal. That careful she got—that careful! It's a bay, the little one. Well, that's that,' Trofim concluded.

The squadron commander gripped his copper mug of tea much as he might the hilt of his sabre when riding into attack. Sleepily, he watched the lamp, where moths danced wildly around the yellow tongue of flame. They came in through the open window, to dance a while and then dash themselves to death against the hot glass, while others came to take their place.

'Bay or black—what's the difference?' the squadron commander said. 'You'll have to shoot it anyway. Are we gypsies, or what, to drag a foal around with us? Eh?.. Well, as I was saying—are we gypsies? Suppose the commander comes along to inspect the regiment—and this foal of yours frisks around, spoiling the formation? What then? We'd be disgraced before the whole Red Army! I can't understand, Trofim, how you could let this happen. Such laxity, right in the midst of the Civil War! You ought to be ashamed of yourself! The horse-minders have strict orders to keep the stallions apart.'

When Trofim went out of doors next morning, carrying his rifle, the sun was not yet up, and the dew glowed rosily on the grass. The meadow, trampled by infantry boots and criss-crossed with trenches, had the look of a girl's face, young but tear-stained and already lined with grief. In the yard, the kitchen orderlies were preparing breakfast. On the doorstep sat the squadron commander in his sweat-stiffened undershirt, plaiting a wickerwork skimmer. His hands, more used of late to the bracing cold of his revolver than to the once familiar household tasks, kept fumbling at their work.

'What's that you're making—a skimmer?' Trofim asked, passing by.

'Ah, it's the woman here—keeps after me all the time,' the squadron commander muttered, working a twig around the handle. 'I used to be good at this sort of thing, but I've lost the knack.'

'Looks all right to me,' Trofim returned.

The squadron commander brushed the left-over twigs from his lap.

'Off to shoot that foal?' he inquired.

Trofim shrugged silently and went on towards the stable.

The squadron commander sat with bowed head, waiting for the shot. But minute after minute passed, and no shot sounded. And then Trofim reappeared from behind the stable, looking rather uncomfortable.

'Well, what's up?'

'Reckon like the firing pin's stuck. Keeps misfiring.'

'Let me have a look.'

Reluctantly, Trofim handed over his rifle. The squadron commander slid open the bolt.

92

'It isn't loaded,' he said.

'You don't say!' Trofim exclaimed, a bit too earnestly.

'It's empty, I tell you.'

'Oh! Well, I'd better tell you. I emptied it. Behind the stable.'

The squadron commander put down the gun. For some time he said nothing, mechanically fingering the wicker skimmer he had just finished. The fresh twigs were sticky and fragrant, tickling his nostrils with the odour of flowering willow, and the smells of freshly turned soil long forgotten in the raging flames of war.

'Damn it all!' he said. 'Let it live. For the time being, at least. Some day, maybe, when the war is over, it will pull a plough for someone. And the commander—well, he'll see how it is, because what has a suckling to do but suck; we've all done it, even the commander. So that's that. And there's nothing wrong with your gun.'

* * *

A month or so later, near the village of Ust-Khopyorskaya, Trofim's squadron went into battle with a company of Cossacks. It was late afternoon when the skirmishing began, and dusk was gathering by the time the squadron charged. Trofim soon fell hopelessly behind his unit. Neither the lash nor the bit, tearing at her lips until they bled, could make his mare join in the charge. Throwing back her head and neighing hoarsely, she stood nervously stamping her feet, until the foal came scampering up, its tail flying. His face distorted with anger, Trofim dismounted, sheathed his sabre, and tore the rifle from his shoulder. At the edge of the bluff, the squadron's

93

right flank had already closed with the enemy. Back and forth the mass of horsemen swayed, as though rocked by the wind, slashing away in a grim silence broken only by the rumble of the horses' hoofs. Trofim threw a swift glance at the struggling men, then turned and took a hasty aim at the foal's finely-shaped head. But his hand must have jerked when he pressed the trigger, or perhaps it was something else that spoiled his shot. At any rate, the foal only kicked out playfully, gave a shrill neigh, and dashed off in a circle, scattering little grey clouds of dust. Then, some distance away, it stopped and stood still. Trofim emptied his gun at the little imp— red-tipped armour bullets, too, which had been the first to come to hand in his cartridge pouch. But the bullets did no harm to the foal. Cursing savagely, Trofim remounted his mare and rode as fast as it would take him to help the squadron commander and three of his men, who were hard pressed by the bearded, red-faced Cossack old-believers.

The squadron camped, that night, by a shallow gully in the steppe. There was little smoking, and the horses were not unsaddled. A patrol sent to the river bank reported that the enemy had amassed considerable forces at the crossing.

His bare feet wrapped in the folds of his waterproof, Trofim lay half asleep, looking back over the events of the day. Again he saw the squadron commander leaping down the steep bank, and the toothless Old-Believer slashing crosswise at the commissar, and the thin little Cossack lad someone had cut to pieces, and somebody's saddle, black with blood; yes, and that foal...

Towards morning the squadron commander came up to Trofim and squatted by his side.

'Asleep, Trofim?'

'Dozing.'

Looking away at the fading stars, the squadron commander said,

'Shoot that foal of yours. It's bad for morale. The very sight of it makes me so soft I can't use my sabre. You see, it reminds us of home, and that's no good in war. Turns your heart from stone to mush. Did you notice—the little imp was right in the thick of it, and never got a scratch.'

The squadron commander broke off for a moment, his lips touched by a dreamy smile. But Trofim didn't see this smile.

'Its tail, Trofim! Have you noticed how it throws it up and skips away with it streaming in the wind. Like a fox's tail, I swear. A beauty of a tail!'

Trofim did not answer. He drew his coat up over his head, shivered with the damp of the dew, and fell quickly asleep.

* * *

Opposite an ancient monastery, a hill jutted out from the right bank, and the Don rushed through the narrows in headlong fury. At the bend the water seethed and bubbled, and green, crested waves flung themselves against the chalky boulders that marked the site of a spring landslide.

The squadron commander would never normally have ordered a crossing opposite the monastery; but where the river was broader and more peaceful, and the current weaker, the bank was held by the Cossacks, and the hill kept under fire.

The crossing began at noon. A makeshift raft took one of the machine-gun carts complete with crew and horses. In midstream the raft swung sharply round against the current and tipped slightly to one side. The left trace-horse, unaccustomed to river crossings, was seized with panic. The squadron, unsaddling in the shelter of the hill, clearly heard its uneasy snorting and the clatter of its hoofs against the sides of the raft.

'It'll sink the raft!' Trofim muttered glumly. His arm, half raised to the mare's sweaty back, fell to his side. With a wild neigh, the frightened horse on the raft jibbed and reared.

'Shoot it!' the squadron leader bellowed.

And, as Trofim watched, the gunner sprang to the neck of the rearing horse and thrust a revolver into its ear. The shot came faintly to the bank, like the report of a child's popgun. The other two horses on the raft pressed closer to one another. To keep the raft balanced, the gun crew shoved the dead horse over against the back of the cart. Slowly, its forelegs crumpled and its head sank down.

Some ten minutes later the squadron commander rode his dun mount into the water, and with a terrific splashing a hundred and eight half-naked men and an equal number of multi-coloured horses followed. The saddles were loaded into three small boats. Trofim steered one of these, leaving his mare with the troop leader Nechepurenko. Half-way across he glanced back and saw the leading horses, already knee-deep, lower their heads reluctantly to drink. Half-whispering, the men urged their horses on. Soon the river a few yards from the bank was thick with snorting horses' heads. The men swam beside their mounts, grasping the horses' manes and holding high above their heads their rifles, to which they had fastened their clothing and their cartridge pouches.

Trofim dropped his oar and stood up in the boat. Screwing up his eyes against the sun, he anxiously scanned the swimming horses for a glimpse of his chestnut mare. The squadron resembled a flight of wild geese scattered across the sky by a sudden shot. The squadron leader's dun led the way, its gleaming haunches rising high above the water. Two silvery-white spots just behind its tail marked the ears of the horse that had belonged to the commissar. The rest followed in a broad, dark mass. And last of all, falling further and further behind, bobbed the shaggy head of the troop leader Nechepurenko and, to his left, the pointed ears of Trofim's mare. Still further back, Trofim with difficulty made out the foal. It was swimming unsteadily, now half out of the water, now immersed right up to its nostrils.

And then the wind, sweeping over the river, brought to Trofim's ear the animal's faint, gossamer-thin call for aid, 'Eee-ooo!'

Clear and sharp as a sabre-tip, the cry stabbed Trofim straight to the heart. The effect on him was startling. He had survived five years of war, had flirted with death many a time, and had never lost his self-control. Yet now his face turned ashy-pale beneath the reddish bristle of his beard, and, snatching up his oar, he swung the boat across the current towards the whirlpool in which the exhausted foal was struggling. The mare too, neighing hoarsely, was swimming to the rescue, and try as he might, Nechepurenko could not restrain her.

'Don't be daft,' cried Trofim's friend, Steshka Yefremov, perched on a heap of saddles in the boat. 'Make for the bank. The Cossacks are coming!'

'Shut your mouth!' Trofim breathed, reaching for his rifle.

The foal had been carried far downstream, and was caught in a small whirlpool that swung it effortlessly round and round, licking at its sides with green-combed waves. Trofim rowed feverishly, jerking the boat from side to side. On the right bank of the

97

river the Cossacks emerged from the shelter of the bluff, and a Maxim gun began its staccato chatter, bullets hissing as they struck the water. An officer in a torn canvas shirt shouted something, waving his revolver.

The foal's cries were fewer now, and fainter, and bore a horrifying resemblance to the cries of a human child. Nechepurenko abandoned the mare and made swiftly for the left bank. Shuddering, Trofim raised his gun and fired into the whirlpool, aiming a little below the foal's head. Then, with a dull moan, he tore off his boots and plunged into the water.

On the right bank, the officer in the canvas shirt shouted, 'Cease fire!'

Within five minutes Trofim had reached the foal and thrust his left arm under its chilled belly. Choking and spluttering, he swam for the left bank. Not a shot sounded from the enemy bank.

The sky, the woods, the sand—everything was green and shadowy. With a last, almost superhuman effort, Trofim reached the shore and dragged the dripping foal out of the water. For a while he lay there, scrabbling at the sand and throwing up the green river water he had swallowed. The voices of his comrades sounded in the wood, and far off beyond the bend cannon were firing. The chestnut mare came up and stood beside Trofim, shaking the water off herself and licking the foal. Glittering drops of water rolled down her limp tail, on to the sand.

Trofim rose unsteadily to his feet and moved away across the sand. He took only a step or two, however, before he staggered and fell. Something hot had pierced his chest, and as he fell he heard the shot. One shot, in the back, from the right bank. Over there, on the right bank, the officer in the torn canvas shirt calmly ejected the smoking cartridge from his gun. Trofim lay dying on the sand, only a step or two from the foal. A blood-stained froth brought the semblance of a smile to his blue, hardset lips that for five long years had not kissed his children.

1926

A DIFFERENT BREED*

The first snow came on the first day of Advent. That night the wind blew from across the Don, rustling the withered red grass in the steppe, piling up the snow in shaggy drifts and licking bare the knobbly spines of the roads.

Night swaddled the stanitsa in a greenish, twilit stillness. Beyond the farmyards the unploughed steppe dozed under a snaggling growth of scrub.

At midnight a wolf began to howl in the ravine, the village dogs barked back, and Old Gavrila awoke. He sat with his legs dangling from the ledge above the stove, clung to the chimney-piece and coughed. And when he had done coughing he spat and groped for his pouch.

Every night, after first cock-crow, the old man would awake and sit smoking and coughing, wheezily loosening the phlegm from his lungs, and in the intervals between these choking fits, the thoughts would wend their well-trodden way through his head. And these thoughts were all of his son, who had not come back from the war.

It was his only son, the first and the last. For

*English translation ©Progress Publishers 1975.

that son Gavrila had worked unsparingly. When the time came to send him off to the front to fight the Reds, he had taken two pairs of oxen to market and on the proceeds bought from a Kalmyk a cavalry horse that was no mere horse but a real whirlwind of the steppe. He had taken a saddle out of the family chest and grandfather's bridle with silver trappings. And at parting he had said, 'Well, Petro, I've equipped you well. Even an officer wouldn't be ashamed to be seen in an outfit like yours. Serve the Cossack Army as your father served it and mind you don't disgrace the quiet Don. Your grandfathers and great-grandfathers did their service for the tsars, and so must you!'

And now Old Gavrila stared through the window, all green with splashes of moonlight, listened to the wind groping in the yard for what did not belong to it, and remembered the days that were gone for ever.

At the send-off party the Cossacks shook the rafters of Gavrila's rush-thatched house with an old Cossack song:

> *We fight and our formation never wavers.*
> *Orders we obey with all our might.*
> *At a word from our commander fathers*
> *We ride out with sword and lance to fight.*

Petro had sat at the table, drunk and so pale that his face seemed almost blue. And when he drained the final, "stirrup cup", he had closed his eyes wearily; but somehow he had managed to mount his horse and sit firm in the saddle. After adjusting his sabre, he had leaned out of the saddle and scooped up a handful of the home soil to take with him. Where did he lie now and what soil had he found in foreign lands to warm his breast?

The old man's coughing was long and dry, the bellows in his chest wheezed and trumpeted up and down the scale, and in moments of respite, when he had cleared his throat and was leaning his bent back against the chimney-piece, his thoughts wended their familiar, well-trodden way through his head.

A month after Old Gavrila had seen off his son, the Reds arrived. They broke into time-hallowed Cossack tradition like an invading enemy and turned the old man's habitual way of life inside out, like an empty pocket. While Petro was on the other side of the Don, zealously earning his sergeant's stripes in battle, back in the village Gavrila fostered, cozened and nursed, just as he had once nursed the flaxen-haired Petro, an old man's brooding hatred of the Reds, of the upstarts from Moscow.

Just to spite them, he wore his breeches with their red stripes, the symbol of Cossack freedom, stitched firmly in black thread to the generously cut woolen cloth. He put on his long Cossack tunic with its Guardsman's orange braid and the marks of the sergeant-major's stripes that had once been there. He loaded his chest with the medals and crosses he had won for serving the monarch faithfully and well; and on Sundays he walked to church with his coat flung open for all to see them.

The chairman of the Soviet that now governed the stanitsa said one day on meeting him: 'Take off the gongs, Grandad! That's out of order nowadays.'

Old Gavrila flared up like gunpowder.

'Who're you to order me about? Did ye give 'em to me?'

'The man who did has been quartermastering for the worms a good long time, I reckon.'

'Let him be then! I'll take off nothing! And nor will you, unless you'd strip a dead man.'

'You're talking too big, Grandad. I was just giving you a bit of friendly advice. You can go to bed with 'em on for all I care. But what about the dogs? They'll be after them pants of yours, you know. They've forgotten what your kind look like, they won't know their own man.'

The insult was as bitter as flowering wormwood. He took off his medals, but the resentment grew like a weed in his soul and began to mate with the hatred that was already there.

Now that he had lost his son, there was no one to work and save for. The barns started falling apart, the cattle broke up their pens, the rafters of the calf-shed that had been ripped open by a storm began to rot. In the stable the mice took over the empty stalls and the reaper grew rusty in its shed.

Most of the horses had gone with the Cossacks, the rest had been commandeered by the Reds, and the only one that they had left behind in exchange, a shaggy-legged, long-eared nag, had been snapped up at once in autumn by Makhno's anarchists. In compensation they had left Gavrila a pair of British puttees.

'Let ours be yours!' the Makhno machine-gunner proclaimed with a wink. 'Get rich, Granfer, out of our pockets.'

All that he had saved and hoarded over the years went to rack and ruin. He could not lift a finger to do anything; but in the spring, when the fallow steppe lay at his feet in languorous submission, the earth tempted the old man and at night he heard its compelling silent call. Unable to resist, he harnessed his oxen to the plough, sliced open the steppe with steel and sowed the black earth's insatiable womb with good wheat.

Cossacks came home from the sea and from across the sea, but no one knew what had happened to Petro. Men had served in different regiments and fought in different parts—Russia is a big place—and it was said that Petro's regiment had been wiped out to the last man in an engagement with a Red detachment somewhere on the Kuban.

Gavrila hardly ever spoke to his wife about their son.

At night he would hear her crying and snuffling in her pillow.

'What is it, old woman?' he would say, clearing his throat.

And she would wait a little while before responding.

'It must be the fumes from the stove. I've got a headache.'

And he would pretend not to know what the real trouble was.

'Why don't you drink some pickle-juice? I'll go down to the cellar and get you some.'

'Go to sleep, man. It'll pass.'

And once again the stillness would spread its invisible web over the house. And the moon would stare in arrogantly through the window, enjoying the sight of another's grief, the sorrow that breaks a mother's heart.

But still they waited and hoped for their son's return. When Gavrila decided to have some sheepskin dressed, he said to his wife, 'We'll manage as we are, but what will Petro wear when he comes home? Winter's on the way, we must make him a coat.'

So they had a coat made to fit Petro and put it away in the chest. They also made him a pair of working boots, for cleaning out the cattle-shed.

The old man took good care of his own fine blue uniform and sprinkled it with tobacco to save it from the moth. And when they killed a lamb, Gavrila made a tall hat out of the skin and hung it on a nail. And when he came in from the yard, the sight of it would bring him up short, as if he were expecting Petro to step smilingly from the front room with a 'Well, Dad, is it cold outside?'

About two days later he went out just before dusk to clean the cattle-shed. He had thrown some hay into the mangers and was about to draw water from the well, when he remembered that he had left his mittens indoors. So he went back to the house, opened the door and there he saw his old wife kneeling on the floor by the bench, holding the hat that Petro had never worn to her breast and nursing it like a baby.

Everything went dark before his eyes. He flung himself at her like a wild beast, knocked her to the floor and, swallowing back the foam that rose to his lips, croaked: 'Stop it! Stop it, you hag! What d'ye mean by it?!'

He snatched the hat away from her, threw it into the chest and fastened the lock. Afterwards he noticed that the old woman's left eye had begun to twitch and her mouth was twisted a little to one side.

The days and weeks flowed by like the waters of the Don, which in autumn are clear and green and always swift.

One day the creeks froze. A belated flock of wild geese flew over the stanitsa, and in the evening the neighbour's boy came over with a message for Gavrila. The boy crossed himself hastily in front of the icon.

'Good-day to you.'

'Praise the Lord.'

'Have you heard, Grandad? Prokhor Likhovidov has come back from Turkey. He was in the same regiment as your Petro.'

Gavrila almost ran down the lane, breathless from coughing and hurrying. But Prokhor was not at home. He had gone away to a neighbouring village to see his brother, promising to return the following day.

There was no sleep for Gavrila that night. He tossed restlessly on the stove-bed, wide awake.

Before daybreak he lighted a rush lamp and started mending his felt boots.

Morning—a pallid weakling—brought a feeble dawn from the blue-grey east. The moon was still dozing in the middle of the sky, not even strong enough to take the last few steps to a cloud where it could shelter for the day.

Before breakfast-time Gavrila glanced out of the window.

'Prokhor's coming!' he said, for some reason in a whisper.

The man who entered the room did not look like a Cossack at all, his whole appearance was that of a stranger. On his feet he wore a squeaky pair of iron-tipped British boots, and an oddly cut overcoat, evidently not his own, hung baggily from his shoulders.

'Greetings, Gavrila Vasilich!'

'The Lord be praised, soldier! Come in and sit down.'

Prokhor took off his cap, greeted the old woman, and sat down on a bench in the front corner.

'What weather we're having! This wind has snowed us up. You can't get through the drifts.'

'Ay, the snow's early this year. In the old days

106

the cattle would still be out grazing at this time of year.'

There was a painful silence. Gavrila, outwardly composed and firm, said: 'You've aged, lad, in foreign parts.'

Prokhor smiled. 'Nothing there to make a man any younger, Gavrila Vasilich!'

The old woman tried to put in a word.

'Our Petro...'

'Be quiet, woman!' Gavrila snapped. 'Give a man a chance to recover after being out in the frost. You'll have time to find out what you want to know.'

He turned back to his guest.

'Well, Prokhor Ignatich, how's life been treating you?'

'Nothing to boast of. Limped home like a dog with its backside out of joint, and lucky to have managed that.'

'I see. So life was bad with the Turks, was it?'

'Hardly kept body and soul together.' Prokhor drummed on the table with his fingers. 'But you've aged a good deal yourself, Gavrila Vasilich. That's pretty good sprinkling of grey you've got on your head... How do you find life under Soviet rule?'

'I'm waiting for my son, waiting for him to come back and feed us old folk,' Gavrila said, and smiled wryly.

Prokhor hastily averted his eyes. Gavrila noticed this and asked straight out, 'Where is Petro, tell us?'

'You mean you haven't heard?'

'We've heard many different tales,' Gavrila said curtly.

Prokhor twisted the dirty fringe of the table-cloth in his fingers. It was some minutes before he answered.

'In January, I think... Yes, in January, our squadron was stationed near Novorossiisk. That's a town on the sea. And we were carrying on as usual like...'

Gavrila leaned forward. 'Is he dead?' he asked in a low whisper.

Prokhor said nothing and kept his eyes down, as though he had not heard the question.

'Well, we were stationed there and the Reds were trying to break through to get to the mountains and link up with the Greens. So the Squadron Commander puts him—you Petro, that is—in charge of a patrol... Our Commander was Captain Senin... Well, then it happened...'

There was a thud by the stove as a metal cooking pot fell to the floor. The old woman was feeling her way with outstretched arms towards the bed, her throat bursting with the cry she dared not utter.

'Don't howl!' Gavrila rapped threateningly. He planted his elbows firmly on the table and looked Prokhor straight in the eyes. 'Tell us the rest, then,' he said slowly and wearily. 'They cut Petro down... killed him... We'd halted near a wood to give the horses a rest. He'd just loosened his saddle girth and the Reds came at us out of the wood...' The words seemed to choke Prokhor, and he crushed his cap with trembling hands. 'Petro grabbed his saddle-bow and down it went under the horse's belly... She went off like a shot and he couldn't hold her, so ... so he was left behind... And that was that!'

'But suppose I don't believe this?' Gavrila said very slowly and clearly.

Prokhor walked hurriedly to the door without looking round.

'Just as you like, Gavrila Vasilich, but it's true...

I'm telling you the truth, the naked truth... I saw it happen with my own eyes.'

'But suppose I don't want to believe it?' Gavrila gasped out, going purple in the face. His eyes were bloodshot and full of tears. He tore open his shirt and with his hairy chest bare lumbered towards the frightened Prokhor, groaning and tossing back his head. 'Kill my only son?! Our only help! My Petro?! You lying son-of-a-bitch! You're lying, d'ye hear?! Lying! I won't believe it...'

That night he threw his coat over his shoulders, went out into the yard and crunched through the snow in his felt boots to the threshing yard. He stopped by a rick.

The wind was blowing from the steppe, carrying powderly flakes of snow; a black, forbidding darkness was heaped under the bare cherry-trees.

'Son!' Gavrila called softly. He waited a little and, without moving or turning his head, called again: 'Petro! My son!'

Then he lay down with his face in the trampled snow by the rick and closed his eyes in grief.

There had been talk in the stanitsa of the requisitioning of grain, and of the bandits that were moving up country from the lower reaches of the Don. At public meetings called by the Executive Committee the news was whispered around, but Old Gavrila had never set foot on the rickety committee-house steps and had never felt the need. So there was much that he did not hear and that he knew nothing about. It was a great surprise to him when the chairman called on him one Sunday after morning service, accompanied by three men in skimpy tan-coloured sheepskins and carrying rifles.

The chairman shook hands with Gavrila, then let

him have it, like a blow on the head from behind:

'Come on, Grandad, own up! Got any grain?'

'What d'ye think we live on—nowt but the holy spirit?'

'Don't snarl! Tell us where your grain is.'

'In the barn, of course.'

'Show us.'

'Kindly tell me what business you have with my grain?'

A big fair-haired fellow—a high-up of some sort, by the look of him—stamped his feet in the cold and said: 'We're collecting all surpluses for the state. Food requisitioning. Haven't you heard about it, Dad?'

'And suppose if I won't give you any?' Gavrila said hoarsely, swelling with anger.

'We'll take it without asking!'

The chairman and his men whispered among themselves and climbed into the corn bins, leaving clots of snow from their boots on the clean golden-brown wheat. The fair-haired man lit a cigarette and made his decision.

'Leave 'em enough for sowing, for their own needs and take the rest.' With a proprietary glance he assessed the amount of grain and turned to Gavrila. 'How much land are you going to sow?'

'Not a damn thing!' Gavrila spat out, his face twisting violently as he began to cough. 'Take it and a pox on you! Rob us of all we have! It's yours!'

'Steady there! Steady, Grandad! Are you mad?!' the chairman remonstrated, flapping his mitten at Gavrila.

'Choke yourselves on other people's goods! Eat till you burst!'

The fair-haired man flicked a wet icicle off his moustache, gave Gavrila a shrewd, ironic glance, and said with a calm smile: 'Hold your horses, Grandad! Shouting won't help. What's all the row about, has someone trodden on your tail?' Then his brows came together and his voice suddenly hardened: 'Don't let your tongue run away with you! If it's too long, you'd better tie it to your teeth! The penalty for agitation...' He slapped the yellow holster slung from his belt without finishing the sentence, then added a little more gently: 'Mind you deliver it today.'

The old man didn't actually take fright, but that firm, decisive voice knocked the wind out of him and made him realise that there was nothing to be gained by shouting. With a helpless flip of the hand he walked back to the porch. But before he had covered half the distance he was brought up short by a wild yell:

'Where're these requisitioners?!'

Gavrila swung round. On the other side of the fence a rider had reared his prancing horse. The feeling that something extraordinary was afoot made Gavrila's knees tremble. Before he could open his mouth, the horseman, seeing the men standing outside the barn, backed his horse sharply and with an imperceptibly swift movement of the hand ripped the rifle from his shoulder.

The shot cracked resonantly and in the stillness that for a brief instant fell upon the yard the bolt clicked twice and the cartridge case flew out with a whirr.

The first moment of stupefaction passed. The fair-haired man flattened himself against the doorpost and with agonising slowness his jerking hand drew the revolver from its holster. The chairman scuttled across the yard towards the threshing floor, hopping and squatting like a hare. One of the requisitioners dropped on one knee and emptied his

111

carbine at the black sheepskin cap bobbing above the fence. A volley of shots swept the yard. Gavrila wrenched his feet out of the snow and pounded heavily to the porch. Looking round, he saw the three men in tan-coloured coats stumbling through the snowdrifts towards the threshing barn as a bunch of horsemen poured in through the hospitably open gates.

The leader, in a Kuban hat and riding a bay stallion, was crouched over his saddle-bow and whirling a sabre above his head. The streaming scarves of his white hood flashed in front of Gavrila like swan's wings and the snow from the horse's hooves spattered in his face.

As he sank back weakly against the carved post of the porch, Gavrila saw the bay leap a fence and rear beside a partly used rick of barley straw while its rider leaned out of the saddle and hewed with cross strokes at a writhing requisitioner.

From the threshing floor came the sound of scuffling and a long, sobbing scream. A moment later a single shot rang out. The pigeons, which had only just settled on the roof of the barn after the first burst of firing, swept into the sky again like a violet burst of buckshot. The horsemen on the threshing floor dismounted.

Meanwhile a festive clangour had broken out over the stanitsa. Pasha—the local simpleton—had climbed the belltower and in his foolishness was tugging all the bell-ropes at once, sounding an Eastertide ring-a-ding-dong instead of an alarm.

The leader, in the Kuban hat, strode up to Gavrila, his white hood thrown back over his shoulders. His perspiring face was twitching and there was a trickle of saliva at the drooping corners of his mouth.

'Got any oats?'

Gavrila raised himself with difficulty from the steps. Overwhelmed by what he had seen, he could scarcely move his tongue.

'Are you deaf, you old devil?! Have you any oats, I asked. Bring us a sackful!'

But before they had time to lead their horses to the feeding-trough, another rider dashed in at the gate.

'To horse! Infantry coming down the hill...'

With a curse the leader bridled his steaming, sweatbathed mount and paused only to rub snow on the cuff of his right sleeve, which was thickly smeared with purplish red.

As the five men rode out of the yard Gavrila noticed the blood-stained coat of the fair-haired food-requisitioner strapped to the saddle of the last rider.

The sound of firing in the thorny ravine beyond the hill continued until evening. Stillness skulked in the stanitsa like a beaten dog. The blue dusk was beginning to fall when Gavrila mustered enough courage to go out to the threshing floor. As he stepped through the open wicket-gate he saw the chairman slumped where the bullet had caught him, over one of the hurdles. His arms hung down, as though reaching for his cap, which had dropped off and lay on the ground beyond the hurdle.

On the chaff-sprinkled snow not far from the rick the three requisitioners lay in a row, stripped to their underclothes. As he stared down at them in horror, Gavrila no longer felt the hatred that had dwelt there in the morning. It seemed unreal, a horrible dream, that on his threshing floor, which his neighbour's goats were always plundering for

113

wisps of straw, there should now lie these butchered bodies, with the odour of death and decay already rising from them and the half-frozen pools of frothy blood.

The fair-haired man lay with his head turned awkwardly sideways and but for that head, firmly embedded in the snow, one might have thought he was resting, so carelessly were his legs crossed one over the other.

The second man, with a black moustache and some of his front teeth missing, was lying with his back arched and his head pulled into his shoulders, his lips drawn back in an unrelenting snarl of fury. The third, who had plunged headlong into the straw, seemed to be swimming across the snow, so much strength and effort was there in the death-stilled sweep of his arms.

Gavrila bent over the fair-haired one, peering into his ashen face, and gave a start of pity. Before him lay not a fierce, prickly-eyed food-requisitioning commissar, but a lad of nineteen. Hoarfrost and little lines of sadness were congealing under the yellow fluff of his moustache and only the forehead was creased by a deep stern furrow.

Aimlessly Gavrila let his hand fall on the lad's bare chest—and drew back in surprise. Through the icy chill his palm had sensed a dying warmth...

His old wife gasped and backed away ·to the stove, crossing herself, when Gavrila staggered in groaning with the stiff blood-blackened body on his back.

He laid the body on the bench, washed it with cold water and began rubbing the chest, arms and legs with a rough woolen sock. He rubbed until he was tired, till the sweat broke out on his forehead. Then he placed his ear to that repellently cold chest and was just able to hear the muffled, faltering beat of the heart.

For three days and four nights he had been lying in the front room, yellow and pale as a corpse. A purple, blood-encrusted scar ran across his forehead and cheek, and his tightly bandaged chest heaved under the blanket, taking breath with a wheezy gurgle.

Every day Gavrila parted his lips with a cracked and calloused finger and prised open the clenched teeth with the tip of a knife while his wife poured warm milk and mutton broth into his mouth through a reed.

On the morning of the fourth day a flash appeared in the lad's cheeks and by noon his face was flaming like a hawthorn bush, fired by frost; his whole body began to shake violently and cold, sticky sweat oozed forth under his shirt.

From the moment he began to murmur in delirium, trying to rise from the bed. Gavrila and the old woman took turns to watch over him day and night.

Through the long winter nights, when the east wind from across the Don stirred the black sky and spread the cold clouds low over the village, Gavrila would sit at the wounded man's bedside with his head sunk in his hands, listening to him muttering some incoherent tale in that strange broad accent of his. He would stare at the dark triangle of sunburn on his chest, at the blue lids of the closed eyes, rimmed with horse-shoes of grey, and when a long drawn-out moan, a gruff command or foul abuse poured from the faded lips and the face became contorted with pain and anger, Gavrila felt the hot tears welling in his throat, and at such moments pity came unbidden.

Gavrila noticed that with every day, with every sleepless night at the sick man's bedside his wife grew paler and more drawn; he noticed the tears on her furrowed cheeks and understood, or rather sensed with his heart, that her love for her dead son Petro, buried deep within her along with the tears she had not been able to shed, had spread like wild-fire to this motionless, death-kissed boy, another woman's son...

The commander of a regiment that passed through the village came to the house one day. He left his horse with an orderly at the gate and ran up the steps to the porch with clanking sword and spurs. In the front room he took off his cap and for a long time stood silent by the bed. Pale shadows stirred on the wounded man's face, a trickle of blood oozed from his lips, which were charred black with fever. The commander shook his prematurely grey head and stared mistily past Gavrila, evading the old man's eyes.

'Look after our comrade, old man!' he said.

'We will!' Gavrila replied firmly.

The days lengthened into weeks. Christmas came and went. On the sixteenth day the lad opened his eyes and Gavrila heard a cracked voice, thin as a spider's web, say:

'Is that you, old man?'

'It is.'

'Make a nice mess of me, did they?'

'Christ save us!'

Gavrila fancied that in that brief, transparent glance he caught a gleam of simple, unmalicious humour.

'What about the other boys?'

'Them... We buried 'em on the square.'

The lad's fingers moved over the blanket and, without saying anything, he shifted his glance to the

116

rough-timbered ceiling.

'What's your name?' Gavrila asked.

The blue-veined eyelids drooped wearily.

'Nikolai.'

'Well, we'll call you Petro... We had a son called Petro,' Gavrila explained.

He thought for a moment and was about to ask something else, but the sound of steady breathing, through the nose, stopped him and, holding out his arms for balance, he tiptoed away from the bed.

Life returned to him slowly, reluctantly. After a month he managed with an effort to lift his head from the pillow; bed-sores appeared on his back.

As the days went by, Gavrila sensed with dismay that he was becoming more and more attached to the new Petro, while the image of the first, his own son, was fading, growing dim like the gleam of the setting sun on the mica windows of his cottage. He tried to revive his former grief and anguish, but what had once been so near was drifting farther and farther away, and it made him feel awkward and ashamed... He would go out and spend hours pottering in the yard, but when he remembered that his wife had all this time been sitting at Petro's bedside, he would be overcome by jealousy. Going indoors, he would stand silently at the head of the bed, straighten the pillow with his stiff fingers and, feeling the old woman's angry glance upon him, sit down on the bench and keep quiet.

His wife fed Petro on marmot fat and an infusion of herbs, picked in spring, in the full bloom of May. Either because of this or because youth had got the better of decay, the wounds healed, the lad's cheeks

117

filled out and reddened with fresh blood and only the right forearm, where the bone had been splintered, failed to mend properly; evidently its working days were over.

In the second week of Lent, however, Petro managed to sit up in bed without assistance. He seemed surprised at his own strength and his face broke into a broad, incredulous smile.

That night in the kitchen the old man's voice came amid coughs from the stove:

'You asleep, old one?'

'What's the matter?'

'Our boy will be getting up soon... You'd better get Petro's breeches out of the chest tomorrow... Get a full outfit ready for him... The lad's got nothing to wear.'

'I know. I've got them out already.'

'You're quick, woman! Did you get his coat out too?'

'And why not? Is the boy to go about naked?'

Gavrila turned over once or twice on the stove and was about to doze off, when he remembered something else and triumphantly raised his head.

'What about the hat? You forgot the hat, I'll be bound, you old goose?'

'Oh, leave me alone! You've passed by it forty times without seeing it. It's been hanging on yon nail since yesterday!'

Gavrila coughed in annoyance and fell silent.

A bustling spring was already bestirring the Don. The ice looked dark and worm-eaten and was porously swollen. The hill-sides were bare. The snow had retreated from the steppe into the ravines and gullies, the far bank was basking in sunny floodwater, and from the steppe the wind wafted the bitter fragrance of reviving wormwood.

It was the end of March.

'I'll get up today, Father!'

Though all the Red Army men who had crossed the threshold of Gavrila's house had called him father when they saw his grey hair, Gavrila noticed a special warmth in this voice. Perhaps it only seemed so to him, or perhaps Petro really had said the word with filial affection, but Gavrila's face went a rich crimson; he began to cough and, concealing his embarrassed joy, muttered, 'You've had over two months of it... It's about time, Petro.'

Petro hobbled stiffly out on to the porch and almost choked from the abundance of air that the wind poured into his lungs. Gavrila supported him from behind, while his old wife fussed round the porch, wiping away a few of her customary tears on her apron.

As he hobbled past the raggedly thatched barn, their adopted son Petro asked: 'Did you take in the grain, after all?'

'I did,' Gavrila grunted unwillingly.

'You did the right thing, Father!'

And again that word 'Father' warmed Gavrila's heart. Every day Petro hobbled about the yard, leaning on a stick, and from everywhere, from the threshing floor, from the shed, wherever he happened to be, Gavrila watched his new son with anxious, searching eyes, afraid that he might trip and fall.

They spoke little to each other, but a simple, affectionate relationship grew up between them.

About two days after Petro had taken his first walk out of doors, at bed-time, as he was making himself comfortable on the stove, Gavrila asked: 'Where d'ye hail from, son?'

'From the Urals.'

'Peasant stock, eh?'

'No, working class.'

'Now, how'd that be? Did you have a trade of some kind? What were you? A cobbler? Or a cooper, eh?'

'No, Father, I worked at a factory. At an iron foundry. I grew up there.'

'And how did you come to be collecting grain?'

'They sent me from the army.'

'What were you then? One o' their commanders?'

'Yes, Father.'

The next question was hard to ask, but it was what he had been leading up to.

'So you're a Party man then?'

'I'm a Communist,' Petro replied, smiling openly.

And the frank, open smile swept away Gavrila's fear of that foreign-sounding word.

The old woman, who had been waiting for a chance to speak, asked quickly: 'Have you a family, Petro dear?'

'Not a soul in the world. I'm all alone, like the moon in the sky!'

'Are your parents dead?'

'I was only about seven, just a kid... Father was killed in a drunken fight. Mother makes her living on the streets somewhere...'

'Oh, the bitch! So she left you when you were only a poor little mite, did she?'

'She went off with a labour contractor, and I grew up at the factory.'

Gavrila lowered his legs from the stove and for a long time he was silent. Then he began to speak very clearly and slowly.

'Well, son, if you've got no family, you can stay with us... We had a son once, it's after him we call you Petro... But that was a long time ago and now

120

there's only us two old folk to keep ourselves company... We've worried and feared for your life so long; I reckon that's why we've taken to you like this. You may be of a different breed, but our hearts ache for you, same as if you were our own... Stay with us, lad! We'll live on the land together, it's good land here on the Don, rich and generous... We'll set you up and find a wife for you... I've had my life, you can take over the farm. All I ask you is to respect our old age and give us a place at your table until we die... Don't leave us, old folk, Petro...'

A cricket behind the stove kept up a jarring, monotonous chirping.

The shutters moaned in the wind.

'We've been looking out for a wife for you, the old woman and me!' Gavrila winked with forced cheerfulness, but his lips trembled and broke into a pitifully twisted smile.

Petro stared down at the chipped and broken floor, his left hand tapping on the bench. It came at intervals, a low, anxious sound. *Tap-tap! Tap-tap-tap! Tap-tap-tap!*

Evidently he was considering his reply. When he had made up his mind, he stopped tapping and raised his head with a jerk.

'I'll stay with you, Father, gladly, but I won't make much of a worker. My right arm isn't mending properly, darn it! But I'll do what work I can. I'll stay for the summer, then we'll see.'

'And then, mebbe you'll stay for good!' Gavrila concluded.

The spinning-wheel burst into a joyous hum at the push of the old woman's foot, purring with happiness as it wound the fluffy wool on to the spindle.

Perhaps it was singing a lullaby or promising a

121

life of plenty with its drowsy, steady beat—who can say?

In the wake of spring came sun-scorched days, curly and grey with the rich steppeland dust. Fair weather set in. The Don, as rebellious as ever, was ridged high with combing waves. Thaw water fed the outlying farmsteads. The far bank, all green and greyish-white, loaded the air with the honey fragrance of flowering poplars; in the meadows a lake, strewn with the fallen petals of wild apple blossom, shone rosy as the dawn. At night the summer lightning flashed girlish glances across the sky and the nights were as brief as its fiery flickerings. The oxen had no time to recover from their long days of toil. The cattle grazing on the common pasture had moulted and their ribs showed under their patchy fur.

Gavrila and Petro lived together in the steppe for a week. They ploughed, harrowed and sowed, and spent the nights under the wagon, sharing the same sheepskin, but Gavrila said nothing of how firmly, as though by an invisible chain, he was bound to his new son. Fair-haired, gay, hard-working, he overshadowed the image of the other Petro, the one that was dead. Gavrila thought of him less and less. And work left him no time for memories.

But the days crept by with thievish tread. Soon it was mowing time.

One morning Petro spent hours tinkering with the mower. He amazed Gavrila by the skill with which he sharpened the blades in the forge and made fresh sails to replace the old, broken ones. He passed all day in his labours and, when dusk fell, went off to the Executive Committee office to attend a meeting. While he was away Gavrila's wife, who had been down to fetch water, came in with a letter. The envelope was old and greasy. It was addressed, care of Gavrila, to Comrade Kosykh, Nikolai.

Troubled by vague forebodings, Gavrila fingered the envelope with those smudgy letters scrawled across it in ink pencil.

He held it up to the light and stared at it, but the envelope guarded its secret jealously and Gavrila felt an involuntary surge of anger against this letter that had disturbed his customary peace of mind.

He thought of tearing it up, but decided he must pass it on. He met Petro at the gate with the news.

'There's a letter for you, son.'

'For me?'

'Ay. Go in and read it.'

Indoors Gavrila lit the lamp and with watchful, probing eyes scanned Petro's joyful face as he read the letter. Eventually his impatience got the better of him.

'Where's it from?'

'The Urals.'

'And who wrote it?' the old woman asked curiously.

'My mates at the foundry.'

Gavrila was on his guard at once.

'And what do they write about?'

The smile went out of Petro's eyes and he answered reluctantly: 'They want me back at the foundry. They're going to start it up again. It's been idle since 1917.'

'But... Will you go?' Gavrila asked dully.

'I don't know.'

Petro grew gaunt and sallow. At night Gavrila heard him sighing and turning over in his bed. And after much heart-searching he realized that village life was not for Petro, that it was not his calling to ruffle the black earth of the steppe with the plough. The foundry, which had nurtured Petro, would sooner or later claim him back, and once again barren joyless days would hobble by in black procession. How he longed to tear down that hated foundry brick by brick, raze it to the ground, so that the weeds and nettles might grow there and shed their seed upon it!

On the third day of the mowing, when they came back to the camp for a drink of water, it was Petro who spoke first.

'I can't stay, Father! I've got to go back to the foundry. It's pulling me, twisting my heart-strings...'

'Don't you like the life here?'

'It's not that... The foundry belongs to us. When Kolchak advanced, we held out for ten days. Kolchak's men strung up nine of our men as soon as they took the place. And now the workers who came back from the army are trying to get the foundry going again... They're pretty near starving, and their families, too, but they're doing their best... How can I stay here? D'you think my conscience will let me?'

'What help can you be? Your right arm's no good.'

'That's a funny way of talking, Father. They need everyone they can get.'

'Well, I'm not stopping you. Go, if you like!' Gavrila replied, with a show of cheerfulness. 'Pretend to the old woman you'll be coming back. Say you just want to live there a bit, then come back to us. She'll miss you too much otherwise, it'll be the end of her... You're all we have, y'know...'

And, still clinging to a last hope, he went on

124

in a husky whisper: 'Maybe you really will come back, eh? Won't you have pity on our old age? Won't you?'

The wagon creaked, the tugging oxen plodded on, the crumbling chalk rustled softly as it sprinkled off the wheels. Near a roadside cross the winding track along the Don turned left. From the turn there could be seen the churches of the district centre and the fanciful green lacework of orchards and vegetable gardens.

Gavrila had been talking throughout the journey, trying to keep a smile on his face.

'Some girls got drowned in the Don at this spot three years ago. That's what the cross is for.' He pointed his whipstock at the forlorn little roof over the cross. 'And this is where we say good-bye. The road don't go any further, there's been a landslide on the hill. It's about a verst from here to the village. You'll manage that on foot.'

Petro adjusted the bag of provisions that hung from his belt and climbed down from the cart. Stifling his sobs with an effort, Gavrila flung his whip to the ground and held out his trembling arms.

'Good-bye, my boy! The sun won't rise for us without you...' His tearful, anguished face puckered and he suddenly raised his voice to a shout: 'Sure you haven't forgotten your pies, son? The pies the old woman baked for you... Got them, have you? Well, good-bye! Good-bye, laddie!'

Petro set off, limping and almost running, along the narrow verge of the road.

'Come back!' Gavrila called, clutching at the side of the cart.

'He never will!' sobbed a silent voice in his heart.

125

For the last time that dear fair head showed up round the bend, for the last time Petro waved his cap, and where his feet had trodden the wind foolishly began to stir and eddy the smoky-white dust.

1926

THE FATE OF A MAN

"I would like my books to help people become better and purer in heart, to arouse love for man and a desire to become an active fighter for the ideals of humanism and human progress. If I succeeded in some measure, then I am happy."

Mikhail SHOLOKHOV
(From his speech at the presentation of the Nobel Prize)

For Yevgenia Grigoryevna Levitskaya,
member of the CPSU since 1903

There was a rare drive and swiftness in the spring
that came to the upper reaches of the Don in the
first year after the war. At the end of March, warm
winds blew from the shores of the Azov Sea and in
two days the sandy left bank of the river was bare;
in the steppe, the snow-choked gullies and ravines
swelled, the streams burst the ice and flooded madly,
and the roads became almost completely impassable.

At this unfavourable time of the year it so happened that I had to make a journey to the village of
Bukanovskaya. The distance was not great—only
about sixty kilometres—but it turned out to be hard
going. My friend and I set out before sunrise. The
pair of well-fed horses strained at the traces and could
scarcely pull the heavy wagon. The wheels sank axle-
deep into the damp mush of sand mixed with snow
and ice and in an hour creamy-white flecks of foam
appeared on the horses' flanks and thighs and under
the narrow breech bands, and the fresh morning air
was invaded by a sharp, intoxicating smell of sweat
and warm harness lavishly smeared with tar.

Where the going was particularly heavy for the
horses we got out and walked. It was hard to walk
through the slushy snow, which squelched under our
boots, but the roadside was still coated with a glitter-

129

ing crust of ice, and there it was even harder. It took us about six hours to do the thirty kilometres as far as the ford over the River Yelanka.

At the village of Mokhovsky the little river, almost dry in summer, had now spread itself over a full kilometre of marshy water meadows, overgrown with alders. We had to make the crossing in a leaky flat-bottomed boat that could not take more than three people at the most. We sent wagon and horses home. In a collective-farm shed on the other side an old and battered jeep that had been standing there most of the winter was awaiting us. The driver and I, with some misgivings, climbed into the unsteady little craft. My friend stayed behind on the bank with our belongings. We had scarcely pushed off when little fountains of water came spouting up through the rotten planks. We plugged them with anything we could lay hands on and kept bailing until we reached the other side. It took us an hour to reach the far bank of the river. The driver fetched the jeep from the village and went back to the boat.

'If this perishing old tub doesn't fall to bits in the water,' he said, picking up an oar, 'I'll be back with your friend in a couple of hours. At the earliest.'

The village lay a good distance from the river, and down by the water there was the kind of stillness that falls on deserted places only late in autumn or at the very beginning of spring. The air over the water was damp and bitter with the smell of rotting alders, but from the distant steppes bathing in a lilac haze of mist a light breeze brought the eternally young, barely perceptible aroma of earth that has not long been liberated from the snow.

Not far away, on the sand at the water's edge, lay a broken wattle fence. I sat down on it to have a smoke but, when I put my hand in my jacket pocket, I discovered to my dismay that the packet of cigarettes I had been carrying there was soaked. On the way across a wave had slapped over the side of the wallowing boat and splashed me to the waist in muddy water. There had been no time to think of my cigarettes, for I had to drop my oar and start bailing as fast as I could to save us from sinking, but now, vexed at my own carelessness, I drew the sodden packet gingerly out of my pocket, got down on my haunches and began laying out the moist brownish cigarettes one by one on the fence.

In was noon. The sun shone as hot as in May. I hoped the cigarettes would soon dry. It was so hot that I began to regret having put on my quilted army trousers and jacket for the journey. It was the first really warm day of the year. But it was good to sit there alone, abandoning myself completely to the stillness and solitude, to take off my old army cap and let the breeze dry my hair after the heavy work of rowing, and to stare idly at the white big-breasted clouds floating in the faded blue.

Presently I noticed a man come out on the road from behind the end cottages of the village. He was leading a little boy by the hand; about five or six years old he was, I reckoned, not more. They tramped wearily towards the ford, but, on reaching the jeep, turned and came in my direction. The man, tall and rather stooped, came right up to me and said in a deep husky voice,

'Hullo, mate.'

'Hullo.' I shook the big rough hand he offered me.

The man bent down to the little boy and said, 'Say hullo to Uncle, son. Looks as if he's another driver like your dad. Only you and I used to drive a lorry, didn't we, and he goes about in that little bus over there.'

Looking straight at me with eyes that were as bright and clear as the sky, and smiling a little, the boy boldly held out a pink cold hand. I shook it gently and asked, 'Feeling chilly, old man? Why's your hand so cold on a hot day like this?'

With a touching childish trustfulness the boy pressed against my knees and lifted his little flaxen eyebrows in surprise.

'But I'm not an old man, Uncle. I'm only a boy, and I'm not chilly either. My hands are cold because I've been making snowballs.'

Taking the half-empty rucksack off his back, the father sat down heavily beside me and said, 'This passenger of mine is a regular young nuisance, he is. He's made me tired as well as himself. If you take a long stride he breaks into a trot; just you try keeping in step with a foot-slogger like him. Where I could take one pace, I have to take three instead, and so we go on, like a horse and a tortoise. And you need eyes in the back of your head to know what he's doing. As soon as you turn your back, he's off paddling in a puddle or breaking off an icicle and sucking it like a lollipop. No, it's no job for a man to be travelling with someone like him, not on foot anyway.' He was silent for a while, then asked, 'And what about you, mate? Waiting for your chief?'

I didn't want to tell him I was not a driver, so I answered,

'Looks as if I'll have to.'

'Is he coming over from the other side?'

'He will be.'

'Do you know if the boat will be here soon?'

'In about two hours.'

'That's quite a long time. Well, let's take it easy, I'm in no hurry. Just saw you as I was walking past, so I thought to myself, there's one of us, drivers, enjoying a spot of sunshine. I'll go over and have a smoke with him, I thought. No fun in smoking alone, any more than in dying alone. You're doing well,

I see, smoking cigarettes. Get them wet, eh? Well, mate, wet tobacco's like a doctored horse, neither of them any good. Let's have a go at my old shag instead.'

He pulled a worn silk pouch out of the pocket of his thin khaki trousers, and as he unrolled it, I noticed the words embroidered on the corner, 'To one of our dear soldiers, from a pupil of Lebedyanskaya Secondary School.'

We smoked the strong home-grown tobacco and for a long time neither of us spoke. I was going to ask him where he was making for with the boy, and what brought him out on such bad roads, but he got his question in first.

'At it all through the war, were you?'

'Nearly all of it.'

'Front-line?'

'Yes.'

'Well, I had a bellyful of trouble out there too, mate. More than enough of it.'

He rested his big dark hands on his knees and let his shoulders droop. When I glanced at him sideways I felt strangely disturbed. Have you ever seen eyes that look as if they have been sprinkled with ash, eyes filled with such unabating pain and sadness that it is hard to look into them? This chance acquaintance of mine had eyes like that.

He broke a dry twisted twig out of the fence and for a minute traced a curious pattern in the sand with it, then he spoke.

'Sometimes I can't sleep at night, I just stare into the darkness and I think, "What did you do it for, life? Why did you maim me like this? Why did you punish me so?" And I get no answer, either in darkness, or when the sun's shining bright... No, I get no answer, and I'll never get one!'

He checked himself, nudged his little son affec-

133

tionately and said, 'Go on, laddie, go and play down by the water, there's always something for little boys to do by a big river. Only mind you don't get your feet wet.'

While we had been smoking together in silence, I had taken a quick look at father and son and one thing about them had struck me as odd. The boy was dressed plainly but in good stout clothes. The way the long-skirted little coat with its soft lining of worn beaver lamb fitted him, the way his tiny boots had been made to fit snugly over the woollen socks, the very neat darn that joined an old tear on the sleeve of the coat, all these things spoke of a woman's hand, the skilful hand of a mother. But the father's appearance was quite different. His quilted jacket was scorched in several places and roughly darned, the patch on his worn khaki trousers was not sewn on properly, but was tacked on with big, mannish stitches; he was wearing an almost new pair of army boots, but his woollen socks were full of moth holes. They had never known the touch of a woman's hand. Either he's a widower, I decided, or there's something wrong between him and his wife.

He watched his son run down to the water, then coughed and again began to speak, and I listened with all my attention.

'To start with, my life was just ordinary. I'm from the Voronezh Province, born there in 1900. During the Civil War I was in the Red Army, in Kikvidze's division. In the famine of 'twenty-two I struck out for the Kuban and worked like an ox for the kulaks, wouldn't be alive today if I hadn't. But my whole family back home, father, mother and sister, starved to death. So I was left all alone. As for relatives anywhere, I hadn't got a single one, not a soul. Well, after a year I came back from the Kuban, sold up my home and went to Voronezh. First I worked as a carpenter, then I went to a factory and learned to be a fitter. And soon I married. My wife had been brought up in a children's home. She was an orphan. Yes, I got a good woman there! Good-tempered, cheerful, always anxious to please. And smart she was, too—no comparison with me. She had known what real trouble was since she was a kid. I dare say that had an effect on her character. Just looking at her from the side, as you might say, she wasn't all that striking, but, you see, I wasn't looking at her from the side, I was looking straight at her. And for me there was no more beautiful woman in the whole world, and there never will be.

'I'd come home from work tired, and bad-tempered as hell sometimes. But no, she'd never fling your rudeness back at you. She'd be so gentle and quiet, couldn't do enough for you, always trying to make you something nice to eat, even when there wasn't enough to go round. It made my heart lighter just to look at her. After a while I'd put my arm round her and say, "I'm sorry, Irina dear, I was damn rude to you, I had a rotten day at work today." And again there'd be peace between us, and my mind would be at rest. And you know what that means for your work, mate? In the morning I'd be out of bed like a shot and off to the factory, and any job I laid hands on would go like clockwork. That's what it means to have a real clever girl for a wife.

'Sometimes I'd have a drink with the boys on pay-day. And sometimes, the scissor-legged way I staggered home afterwards, it must have been frightening to watch. The main street wasn't wide enough for me, let alone the side streets. In those days I was tough and strong and I could hold a lot of drink, and I always got home on my own. But sometimes the last stretch would be in bottom gear, you know. I'd finish it on my hands and knees. But again I'd never get a word of reproach, no scolding, no shouting. My Irina, she'd just laugh at me, and she did that careful like, so that even drunk as I was I wouldn't take it wrong. She'd pull my boots off and whisper, "You'd better lie next to the wall tonight, Andrei, or you might fall out of bed in your sleep." And I'd just flop down like a sack of oats and everything would go swimming round in front of me. And as I dropped off to sleep, I'd feel her stroking my head softly and whispering kind words, and I knew she felt sorry for me.

'In the morning she'd get me up about two hours before work to give me time to come round. She knew I wouldn't eat anything after being drunk, so she'd get me a pickled cucumber or something like that, and pour me out a good glass of vodka—a hair of the dog, you know. "Here you are, Andrei, but don't do it any more, dear." How could a man let someone down who put such trust in him? I'd drink it up, thank her without words, just with a look and a kiss, and go off to work like a lamb. But if she'd said a word to cross me when I was drunk, if she'd started snapping at me, I'd have come home drunk again, believe me. That's what happens in some families, where the wife's a fool. I've seen plenty of it and I know.

'Well, soon the children started arriving. First there was a little boy, then two girls. And that was when I broke away from my mates. I started taking all my pay home to the wife; we had a fair-sized family by then, and I couldn't afford to drink any more. On my day off I'd have just a glass of beer and let it go at that.

'In 'twenty-nine I got interested in motors, I learned the job and started driving a lorry. And when I got into the way of it I didn't want to go back to the factory. Driving seemed to be more fun. And so

136

I lived for ten years without noticing how the time went by. It was like a dream. But what's ten years? Ask any man over forty if he's noticed how the years have been slipping by. You'll find he hasn't noticed a damned thing! The past is like that distant steppe way out there in the haze. This morning I was crossing it and it was clear all round, but now I've covered twenty kilometres there's a haze over it, and you can't tell the trees from the grass, the ploughland from the meadow.

'Those ten years I worked day and night, I earned good money and we lived no worse than other folk. And the children were a joy to us. All three did well at school, and the eldest, Anatoly, turned out to be so bright at mathematics that he even got his name in one of the Moscow papers. Where he inherited this great gift from, I couldn't tell you, mate. But it was certainly flattering, and I was proud of him; mighty proud I was!

'In ten years we saved up a bit of money and before the war we built ourselves a little cottage with two rooms, a store-room and a covered porch. Irina bought a couple of goats. What more did we want? There was milk for the children's porridge, we had a roof over our heads, clothes on our backs, shoes on our feet, so everything was all right. The only thing was the site, it wasn't a very good place to build. The plot of land I got was not far from an aircraft factory. If my cottage had been somewhere else, my life might have turned out different.

'And then it came—war. The next day I had my call-up papers, and the day after it was "Report to the station". All my four saw me off together: Irina, Anatoly, and my daughters, Nastenka and Olyushka. The kids took it well, though the girls couldn't keep back a tear or two. Anatoly just shivered a bit as if he was cold; he was getting on for seventeen by that time. But my Irina... I'd never seen anything like it in all the seventeen years we'd lived together. My shirt and shoulder had stayed wet all night with her tears, and in the morning she was at it again. We got to the station and I felt so sorry for her I couldn't look her in the face. Her lips were all swollen, her hair was poking out from under her shawl, and her eyes were dull and staring, like someone's who's out of his mind. The officers gave the order to get aboard but she flung herself on my chest, and clasped her hands round my neck. She was shaking all over, like a tree that's being chopped down. The children tried to talk her round, and so did I, but nothing helped. Other women chatted to their husbands and sons, but mine clung to me like a leaf to a branch, and just trembled all the time, and couldn't say a word. "Take a grip on yourself, Irina dear," I said. "Say something to me before I go, at least." And this is what she said, with a sob between every word, "Andrei ... my darling ... we'll never ... never see each other again ... in this world..."

'There was I with my heart bursting with pity for her, and she says a thing like that to me. She ought to have understood it wasn't easy for me to part with her. I wasn't going off to a party either. And I lost my temper! I pulled her hands apart and gave her a push. It seemed only a gentle push to me, but I was strong as an ox and she staggered back about three paces, then came towards me again with little steps, arms outstretched and I shouted at her, "Is that the way to say good-bye? Why do you want to bury me before I'm dead?!" But then I took her in my arms again because I could see she was in a bad way.'

He broke off suddenly and in the silence that followed I heard a faint choking sound. His emotion communicated itself to me. I glanced sideways at him but did not see a single tear in those dead, ashy eyes of his. He sat with his head drooping dejectedly. The big hands hanging limply at his sides were shaking slightly; his chin trembled and so did those firm lips.

'Don't let it get you down, friend, don't think of it,' I said quietly, but he seemed not to hear me. Overcoming his emotion with a great effort, he said suddenly in a hoarse, strangely altered voice.

'Till my dying day, till the last hour of my life I'll never forgive myself for pushing her away like that!'

He fell silent again and for a long time. He tried to roll a cigarette, but the strip of newspaper came apart in his fingers and the tobacco spilled on to his knees. In the end he managed to make a clumsy roll of paper and tobacco, took a few hungry pulls at it, then, clearing his throat, went on.

'I tore myself away from Irina, then took her face in my hands and kissed her. Her lips were like ice. I said good-bye to the kids and ran to the carriage, managed to jump on the steps as it was moving. The train started off very slow, and it took me past my family again. I could see my poor little orphaned kids bunched together, waving their hands and trying to smile, but not managing it. And Irina had her hands clasped to her breast; her lips were white as chalk, and she was whispering something, and staring straight at me, and her body was all bent forward as if she was trying to walk against a strong wind... And that's how I'll see her in my memory for the rest of my life—her hands clasped to her breast, those white lips, and her eyes wide open and full of tears. That's mostly how I see her in my dreams too. Why did I push her away like that? Even now, when I remember it, it's like a blunt knife twisting in my heart.'

'We were drafted to our units at Belaya Tserkov, in the Ukraine. I was given a three-tonner, and that's what I went to the front in. Well, there's no point in telling you about the war, you saw it yourself and you know what it was like to start with. I got a lot of letters from home, but didn't write much myself. Just now and then I'd write that everything was all right and we were doing a bit of fighting. We may be retreating at present, I'd say, but it won't be long before we gather our strength and give the Fritzes something to think about. And what else could you write? Those were grim times and you didn't feel like writing. And I must say I was never much of a one for harping on a pitiful note. I couldn't stick the sight of those slobbering types that wrote to their wives and girl friends every day for no reason at all, just to rub their snot over the paper—oh, it's such a hard life, oh, I might get killed! And so he goes on, the son-of-a-bitch, complaining and looking for sympathy, blubbering away, and he can't understand that those poor women and kids are having just as bad a time of it back home as we are. Why, they were carrying the whole country on their shoulders. And what shoulders our women and children must have had not to give in under a weight like that! But they didn't give in, they stuck it out! And then one of those belly-achers writes his pitiful letter and that just knocks a working woman off her feet. After a letter like that, the poor thing won't know what to do with herself or how to face up to her work. No! That's what a man's for, that's what you're a soldier for—to put up with everything, if need be. But if you've got more woman than man in you, then go and put on a frilled skirt to puff out your skinny arse, so you can look like a woman, at least from behind, and go and weed the beet, or milk the cows, because your kind aren't needed at the

140

front. The stink's bad enough there without you!

'But I didn't get even a year's fighting done. I was wounded twice, but only slightly both times, once in the arm, the second time in the leg. The first was a bullet from an aircraft, the second a chunk of shrapnel. The Germans holed my lorry, top and sides, but I was lucky, mate, at first. Yes, I was lucky all the time until I was real unlucky... I got taken prisoner at Lozovenki in the May of 'forty-two. It was an awkward set-up. The Germans were attacking hard and one of our 122 mm howitzer batteries had nearly run out of ammo. We loaded up my lorry chockful of shells. I worked on the job myself till my shirt was sticking to my back. We had to get a move on, because they were closing in on us; on the left we could hear the rumble of tanks, and firing on the right and in front, and things didn't look too healthy.

' "Can you get through, Sokolov?" asks the commander of our company. He need never have asked. Was I going to sit twiddling my thumbs while my mates got killed? "What are you talking about?" I told him. "I've got to get through, and that's that." "Get cracking then," he says, "and step on it!"

'And step on it I did. Never driven like that before in my life! I knew I wasn't carrying a load of spuds, I knew I had to be careful with the stuff I'd got aboard, but how could I be, when the lads were fighting out there empty-handed, when the whole road was under artillery fire. I did about six kilometres and got pretty near the place. I'd have to turn off the road to get to the hollow where the battery was stationed, and then what did I see? Strike me, if it wasn't our infantry running back across the field on both sides of the highroad with shells bursting among them. What was I to do? I couldn't turn back, could I? So I gave her all she'd got. There was only about a kilometre to go to the battery, I had already turned off the road, but I never reached them, mate. Must have been a long-range gun landed a heavy one near the lorry. I never heard the bang nor anything, just something burst inside my head, and I don't remember any more. How I stayed alive, and how long I lay there by the ditch, I've got no idea. I opened my eyes, but I couldn't get up; my head kept jerking and I was shaking as if I had a fever. Everything seemed dark, something was scraping and grinding in my left shoulder, and my body ached all over as if somebody had been lamming into me for two days running with anything he could lay hands on. I squirmed about on my belly for a long time, and finally I managed to get up. But still I couldn't tell where I was, nor what had happened to me. My memory was clean gone. But I was scared to lie down. I was scared I'd never get up again, so I just stood there swaying from side to side like a poplar in a gale.

'When I came to and had a look round, my heart felt as if someone had got a pair of pliers round it. The shells I'd been carrying were lying about all round me. Not far away was my lorry, all buckled up, with its wheels in the air. And the fighting? The fighting was going on behind me. Yes, behind me!

'When I realized that, and I'm not ashamed to say it, my legs just caved in under me and I fell as if I'd been pole-axed, because I realized I was cut off behind the enemy lines, or to put it plainly, I was already a prisoner of the nazis. That's war for you.

'No, it is not an easy thing to take in, mate, it's not easy to understand the fact that you're a prisoner through no fault of your own. And it takes some explaining to a fellow who's never experienced it himself just what that thing means.

142

'So I lay there and soon I heard the tanks rumbling. Four medium German tanks went by me at full speed in the direction I'd come from. What do you think that felt like? Then came the tractors hauling the guns, and a mobile kitchen, then the infantry, not many of them, not more than a company all told. I'd squint up at them out of the corner of my eye and then I'd press my face into the earth again; it made me sick to look at them, sicker than I can say.

'When I thought they'd all gone past, I lifted my head, and there were six submachine-gunners marching along about a hundred paces away. And as I looked, they turned off the road and came straight towards me, all six of them, without saying a word. Well, I thought, this is it. So I got into a sitting position— I didn't want to die lying down—and then I stood up. One of them stopped a few paces away from me and jerked his gun off his shoulder. And it's funny how a man's made, but at that moment I didn't feel any panic, not even a shiver in my heart, I just looked at him and thought, "It's going to be a short burst. I wonder where he'll place it? At my head or across my chest?" As if it mattered a damn to me what part of my body he made his holes in.

'Young fellow he was, pretty well-built, dark-haired, but his lips were thin as thread, and his eyes had a nasty glint in them. That one won't think twice about shooting me down, I thought. And sure enough, up goes his gun. I looked him straight in the eye and didn't say anything. But another one—a corporal or something, he was older, almost elderly by the look of him—shouted something, then pushed the other fellow aside and came up to me. He babbled something in his own language and bent my right elbow. Feeling my biceps he was. "O-o-oh!" he said, and pointed along the road to where the sun was

143

setting, as much as to say, "Off you go, you mule, and work for our Reich." Thrifty type he was, the son-of-a-bitch!

'But the dark-haired one had got his eye on my boots and they looked a good sound pair. He signed to me to take them off. I sat down on the ground, took off my boots and handed them to him. Fair snatched them out of my hands, he did. So I unwound my footcloths and held them out to him, too, looking up at him from the ground. He shouted and swore, and up went his gun again. But the others just roared with laughter. Then they marched off. The dark-haired one looked round at me two or three times before he got to the road, and his eyes glittered like a wolf-cub's with fury. Anyone would think I'd taken his boots instead of him taking mine.

'Well, mate, there was nothing for it. I went on to the road, let out the longest and hottest Voronezh cuss I could think of, and stepped out westward— a prisoner! But I wasn't much good for walking by that time—a kilometre an hour was all I could do, not more. It was like being drunk. You'd try to go straight and something would just push you from one side of the road to the other. I went on for a bit and then a column of our chaps, from the same division as I'd been in, caught up with me. There were about ten German submachine-gunners guarding them. The one at the front of the column came up to me and, without saying a word, just bashed me on the head with his gun. If I'd gone down, he'd have stitched me to the ground with a burst, but our chaps caught me as I fell and hustled me into the middle of the column and half carried me along for a while. And when I came to, one of them whispered, "Don't fall down for God's sake! Keep going while you've got any strength left, or they'll kill you!" And though I had pretty little strength left, I managed to keep going.

'At sunset the Germans strengthened their guard. They brought up another twenty submachine-gunners in a lorry, and drove us on at a quicker pace. The badly wounded ones that couldn't keep up with the rest were shot down in the road. Two tried to make a break for it, but they forgot that on a moonlit night you can be seen a mile away out in the open; of course, they got it too. At midnight we came to a village that was half burned down. They herded us into a church with a smashed dome. We had to spend the night on the stone floor without a scrap of straw. No one had a greatcoat, so there wasn't anything to lie on. Some of the boys didn't even have tunics, just cotton undershirts. They were mostly NCOs. They had taken off their tunics so they couldn't be told from the rank-and-file. And the men from the gun crews hadn't got tunics either. They had taken them off while working at the guns.

'That night it poured with rain and we all got wet to the skin. Part of the roof had been smashed by a heavy shell or a bomb and the rest of it was ripped up by shrapnel; there wasn't a dry spot even at the altar. Yes, we stood around the whole night in that church, like sheep in a dark pen. In the middle of the night I felt someone touch my arm and ask, "Are you wounded, comrade?" "Why do you ask, mate?" I says. "I'm a doctor. Perhaps I can help you in some way?" I told him my left shoulder made a creaking noise and was swollen and hurt like hell. And he says firmly, "Take off your tunic and under-shirt." I took everything off and he started feeling round my shoulder with his thin fingers. And did it hurt! I gritted my teeth and I says to him, "You must be a vet, not a doctor. Why do you press just where it hurts most, you heartless devil?" But he kept on probing about, and he says to me, angry-like. "Your

145

job's to keep quiet, I won't have you talking to me like that! Hang on, it's going to hurt you properly now." And then he gave my arm such a wrench that I saw stars.

'When I got my senses back I asked him, "What are you doing, you rotten nazi? My arm's broken to bits and you give it a pull like that." I heard him chuckle, then he said, "I thought you'd hit out with your right while I was doing it, but you're a good-tempered chap, it seems. Your arm isn't broken, it was dislocated at the shoulder and I've put it back in its socket. Well, feeling better now?" And sure enough I could feel the pain going out of me. I thanked him so he'd know I meant it, and he went on in the darkness, asking quietly, "Any wounded?" There was a real doctor for you. Even shut up like that, in pitch darkness, he went on doing his great work.

'It was a restless night. They wouldn't let us out even to relieve ourselves. The guard commander had told us they wouldn't when he drove us into the church in pairs. And as luck would have it, one of the Christians among us wanted to go out bad. He kept on saving it up and at last he burst into tears. "I can't pollute a holy place!" he says. "I'm a believer, I'm a Christian. What shall I do, lads?" And you know the kind of chaps we were. Some laughed, others swore, and others started teasing him with all sorts of advice. Cheered us all up, he did, but it turned out bad in the end. He started bashing on the door and asking to be let out. And he got his answer. A nazi gave a long burst through the door with his submachine-gun. It killed the Christian and three more with him, and another was so badly wounded he died by morning.

'We pulled the dead into a corner, then sat down quiet and thought to ourselves, this isn't a very

146

cheerful start. And presently we started whispering to each other, asking each other where we came from and how we'd got taken prisoner. The chaps who'd been in the same platoon or the same company started calling quietly to each other in the darkness. And next to me I heard two voices talking. One of them says, "Tomorrow, if they form us up before they take us on farther and call out for the commissars, Communists, and Jews, you needn't try and hide yourself, platoon commander. You won't get away with it. You think just because you've taken off your tunic you'll pass for a ranker? It won't work! I'm not going to suffer because of you. I'll be the first to put the finger on you. I know you're a Communist, I remember how you tried to get me to join the Party. Now you're going to answer for it." That was the one sitting nearest to me, on the left, and on the other side of him, a young voice answers, "I always suspected there was a bad streak in you, Kryzhnev. Specially when you refused to join the Party, pretending you were illiterate. But I never thought you'd turn out to be a traitor. You went to school until you were fourteen, didn't you?" And the other one answers in a casual sort of way, "Yes, I did. So what?" They were quiet for a long time, and then the platoon commander—I could tell him by his voice—says softly, "Don't give me away, Comrade Kryzhnev." And the other one laughed quietly. "You've left your comrades behind on the other side of the line," he says, "I'm no comrade of yours, so don't plead with me. I'm going to put the finger on you all the same. My own skin comes first with me."

'They stopped talking after that, but the vileness of what I'd heard had given me the shivers. "No," I thought, "I won't let you betray your commander, you son-of-a-bitch. You won't walk out of this church

147

on your own two feet, they'll drag you out by the legs!" Then it began to get light and I could see a fellow with a big fleshy face lying on his back with his hands behind his head, and beside him a little snub-nosed lad, in only an undershirt, sitting with his arms round his knees and looking very pale. "That kid won't be able to handle this great fat gelding," I thought, "I'll have to finish him off myself."

'I touched the lad's arm and asked him in a whisper, "You a platoon commander?" He didn't say anything, just nodded. "That one over there wants to give you away?" I pointed to the fellow lying on his back. He nodded again. "All right," I said, "hold his legs so he won't kick. And be quick about it!" And I jumped on that fellow and locked my fingers round his throat. He didn't even have time to shout. I held him under me for a few minutes, then eased off a bit. That was one traitor less, with his tongue hanging out!

'But I felt rotten afterwards and I wanted to wash my hands something terrible, as if it wasn't a man I'd killed but some crawling snake. It was the first time I had killed anyone in my life, and the man I had killed was one of our own. Our own? No, he wasn't. He was worse than the enemy, he was a traitor. I got up and said to the platoon commander, "Let's get away from here, comrade, the church is a big place."

'In the morning, just as that Kryzhnev had said, we were all lined up outside the church with a ring of submachine-gunners covering us, and three SS officers started trying to pick out the ones among us they thought were dangerous—Communists, officers, and commissars. But they didn't find any. And they didn't find anybody who was swine enough to give them away either, because nearly half of us were Communists, and there were a lot of officers, too, and commissars. Out of over two hundred men they only picked four. One Jew and three Russians from the rank-and-file. The Russians landed in trouble because they were all dark and had curly hair. The SS men just came up to them and said, "Jude?" The one they asked said he was a Russian, but they wouldn't even listen. "Step out!" and that was that.

'They shot the poor devils and drove us on further. The platoon commander who'd helped me strangle that traitor kept by me right as far as Poznan. The first day of the march he'd edge up to me every now and then and press my hands as we went along. At Poznan we got separated. It happened like this.

'You see, mate, ever since the day I was captured I'd been thinking of escaping. But I wanted it to be a sure thing. All the way to Poznan, where they put us in a proper camp, I never got the right kind of chance. But in the Poznan camp it looked as if I'd got what I wanted. At the end of May they sent us out to a little wood near the camp to dig graves for the prisoners that had died—a lot of our chaps died at that time from dysentery. And while I was digging away at that Poznan clay I had a look round and I noticed that two of our guards had sat down to have a bite; the third was dozing in the sun. So I put down my shovel and went off quietly behind a bush. Then I ran for it, keeping straight towards the sunrise.

'They didn't miss me right away, those guards. Where I found the strength, skinny as I was, to cover nearly forty kilometres in one day, I don't know myself. But nothing came of my effort. On the fourth day, when I was a long way from that damned camp, they caught me. There were blood-hounds on my track, and they sniffed me out in a field of unreaped oats.

149

'Daybreak had caught me in the open and it was at least three kilometres to the woods. I was afraid to go on in the daylight, so I lay low in the oats for the day. I crushed a few ears of grain in my hand and was filling my pockets with a supply, when I heard the barking of dogs and the roar of a motor-bike. My heart sank because the dogs kept coming nearer. I lay flat and covered my head with my arms, so they wouldn't bite my face. Well, they came up and it only took them a minute to tear all my rags off me. I was left in nothing but what I was born in. They dragged me about in the oats, and then a big dog got his forepaws on my chest and started making passes at my throat, but he didn't bite straightaway.

'Two Germans came up on motor-bikes. First they beat me up good and proper, then they set the dogs on me. And they tore into me. I was taken back to camp, naked and bloody as I was. They gave me a month in solitary for trying to escape, but I was still alive, I kept alive somehow.

'It's pretty grim, mate, to remember the things I went through as a prisoner, let alone tell you about them. When I remember all we had to suffer out there, in Germany, when I remember all my mates who were tortured to death in those camps, my heart comes up in my throat and it's hard to breathe.

'The way they shifted me about in those two years I was a prisoner! I reckon I covered half of Germany. I was in Saxony, at a silicate plant, in the Ruhr, hauling coal in a mine. I sweated away with a shovel in Bavaria, I had a spell in Thüringen, and the devil knows what German soil I didn't have to tread. There's plenty of different scenery out there, but the way they shot and bashed our lads was the same all over. And those damned bastards lammed into us like no man here ever beat an animal. Punching us,

150

kicking us, beating us with rubber truncheons, or an iron bar if they happened to have one handy, not to mention their rifle butts and sticks.

'They beat you up just because you were a Russian, because you were still alive in the world, just because you worked for them. And they'd beat you for giving them a wrong look, taking a wrong step, for not turning round the way they wanted. They beat you just so that one day they'd knock the life out of you, so you'd choke with your own blood and die of beating. There weren't enough ovens in the whole of Germany, I reckon, for all of us to be shoved into.

'And everywhere we went they fed us the same— a hundred and fifty grams of ersatz bread, made half of sawdust, and a thin swill of swedes. Some places they gave us hot water to drink, some places they didn't. But what's the use of talking, judge for yourself. Before the war started I weighed eighty-six kilograms, and by the autumn I couldn't turn more than fifty. Just skin and bones, and hardly enough strength to carry the bones either. But you had to work, and not say a word, and the work we did would have been a lot too much for a cart-horse, I reckon.

'At the beginning of September they sent a hundred and forty-two of us Soviet prisoners-of-war from a camp near Küstrin to Camp B-14, not far from Dresden. At that time there were about two thousand in that camp. We were all working in a stone quarry, cutting and crushing their German stone by hand. The stint was four cubic metres a day per man, and for a man, mind you, who could hardly keep body and soul together anyway. And then it really started. After two months, out of the hundred and forty-two men in our group there were only fifty-seven left. How about that, mate? Tough going, eh? We hardly had time to bury our own mates, and then there

151

was a rumour in the camp that the Germans had taken Stalingrad and were pressing on into Siberia. It was one thing on top of another. They held us down so we couldn't lift our eyes from the ground, as if we were asking to be put there, into that German earth. And every day the camp guards were drinking and bawling their songs, rejoicing for all they were worth.

'One evening we came back to our hut from work. It had been raining all day and our rags were soaking; we were all shivering from the cold wind and couldn't stop our teeth chattering. There wasn't anywhere to get dry or warm, and we were as hungry as death itself, or even worse. But we were never given any food in the evenings.

'Well, I took off my wet rags, threw them on to my bunk and said, "They want you to do four cubic metres a day, but one cubic metre would be plenty to bury one of us." That was all I said, but, would you believe it, among our own fellows there was one dirty dog who went and reported my bitter words to the camp commandant.

'The camp commadant, or *Lagerführer*, as they called him, was a German called Müller. Not very tall, thick-set, hair like a bunch of tow; sort of bleached all over. The hair on his head, his eyelashes, even his eyes were a kind of faded colour, and he was pop-eyed besides. Spoke Russian like you and me, even had a bit of a Volga accent, as if he'd been born and bred in those parts. And could he swear! He was a terror for it. I sometimes wonder where the bastard ever learned that trade. He'd line us up in front of the block—that's what they called the hut—and walk down the line surrounded by his bunch of SS men with his right hand held back. He wore a leather glove and under the leather there was a strip of lead to protect his fingers. He'd walk down

152

the line and bloody every other man's nose for him. "Inoculation against flu," he used to call it. And so it went on every day. Altogether there were four blocks in the camp, and one day he'd give the first block their "inoculation", next day it'd be the second, and so on. That bastard worked regular, never took a day off. There was only one thing he didn't understand, the fool; before he started on his round he'd stand out in front there, and to get himself real worked up for it, he'd start cursing. He'd stand there cursing away for all he was worth, and, do you know, he'd make us feel a bit better. You see, the words sounded like our own, it was like a breath of air from over there. If he'd known his cursing and swearing gave us pleasure, he wouldn't have done it in Russian, he'd have stuck to his own language. Only one of our fellows, a pal of mine from Moscow, used to get wild with him. "When he curses like that," he says, "I shut my eyes and think I'm in Moscow, having one at the local, and it just makes me dizzy for a glass of beer."

'Well, the day after I said that about the cubic metres, that commandant had me up on the mat. In the evening an interpreter and two guards came to our hut. "Sokolov Andrei?" I answered up. "Outside! Quick march! *Herr Lagerführer* wants to see you." I guessed what he wanted me for. It was curtains. So I said good-bye to my pals—they all knew I was going to my death. Then I took a deep breath and followed the guards. As I went across the campyard, I looked up at the stars and said good-bye to them too, and I thought to myself, "Well, you've had your full dose of torture, Andrei Sokolov, Number 331." I felt somehow sorry for Irina and the kids, then I got over it and began screwing up my courage to face the barrel of that pistol without flinching, like a soldier should, so the enemy wouldn't see how

153

hard it'd be for me at the last minute to part with this life, bad though it was.

'In the commandant's room there were flowers on the window-sill. It was a nice clean place, like one of our clubs. At the table there were all the camp's officers. Five of 'em, sitting there, downing schnapps and chewing bacon fat. On the table there was a big bottle, already open, plenty of bread, bacon fat, soused apples, all kinds of open tins. I took one glance at all that grub, and you wouldn't believe it, but I felt so sick I nearly vomited. I was hungry as a wolf, you see, and I'd forgotten what the sight of human food was like, and now there was all this stuff in front of me. Somehow I kept my sickness down, but it cost me a great effort, to tear my eyes away from that table.

'Right in front of me sat Müller, half-drunk, flicking his pistol from one hand to the other, playing with it. He had his eye fixed on me, like a snake. Well, I stood to attention, snapped my broken-down heels together, and reported in a loud voice like this, "Prisoner-of-war Andrei Sokolov at your service, *Herr Kommandant*." And he says to me, "So, you Russian Ivan, four cubic metres of quarrying is too much for you, is it?" "Yes, *Herr Kommandant*," I said, "it is." "And is one cubic metre enough to make a grave for you?" "Yes, *Herr Kommandant*, quite enough and to spare."

'He gets up and says, "I shall do you a great honour. I shall now shoot you in person for those words. It will make a mess here, so we'll go into the yard. You can sign off out there." "As you like," I told him. He stood thinking for a minute, then tossed his pistol on the table and poured out a full glass of schnapps, took a piece of bread, put a slice of fat on it, held the lot out to me and said, "Before you die, Russian Ivan, drink to the triumph of German arms."

'I had taken the glass and the bread out of his hand, but when I heard those words, something seemed to scald me inside. "Me, a Russian soldier," I thought, "drink to the victory of German arms? What'll you want next, *Herr Kommandant*? It's all up with me anyway. You can go to hell with your schnapps!"

'I put the glass down on the table, and the bread with it, and I said, "Thank you for your hospitality, but I don't drink." He smiles. "So you don't want to drink to our victory? In the case, drink to your own death." What had I got to lose? "To my death and relief from torment then," I said. And with that, I took the glass and poured it down my throat in two gulps. But I didn't touch the bread. I just wiped my lips politely with my hand and said, "Thank you for your hospitality. I am ready, *Herr Kommandant*, you can sign me off now."

'But he was looking at me sharply. "Have a bite to eat before you die," he said. But I said to him, "I never eat after the first glass." Then he poured out a second and handed it to me. I drank the second and again I didn't touch the food. I was staking everything on courage, you see. "Anyway," I thought, "I'll get drunk before I go out into that yard to die." And the commandant's fair eyebrows shot up in the air. "Why don't you eat, Russian Ivan? Don't be shy!" But I stuck to my guns, "Excuse me, *Herr Kommandant*, but I don't eat after the second glass either." He puffed out his cheeks and snorted, and then he gave a roar of laughter, and while he laughed he said something quickly in German, must have been translating my words to his friends. The other laughed, too, pushed their chairs back, turned their big mugs round to look at me, and I noticed something different in their looks, something a bit softer-like.

155

'The commandant poured me out a third glass and his hands were shaking with laughter. I drank that glass slowly, bit off a little bit of bread and put the rest down on the table. I wanted to show the bastards that even though I was half dead with hunger I wasn't going to gobble the scraps they flung me, that I had my own, Russian dignity and pride, and that they hadn't turned me into an animal as they had wanted to.

'After that the commandant got a serious look on his face, straightened the two iron crosses on his chest, came out from behind the table unarmed and said, "Look here, Sokolov, you're a real Russian soldier. You're a fine soldier. I am a soldier, too, and I respect a worthy enemy. I shall not shoot you. What is more, today our gallant armies have reached the Volga and taken complete possession of Stalingrad. That is a great joy for us, and therefore I graciously grant you your life. Go to your block and take this with you for your courage." And he handed me a small loaf of bread from the table, and a lump of bacon fat.

'I clutched that bread to my chest, tight as I could, and picked up the fat in my other hand. I was so taken aback at this unexpected turn of events that I didn't even say thank you, just did a left about-turn, and went to the door. And all the while I was thinking, now he'll blast daylight through my shoulder-blades and I'll never get this grub back to the lads. But no, nothing happened. Again death passed me by and I only felt the cold breath of it.

'I got out of the commandant's room without a stagger, but outside I went reeling all over the place. I lurched into the hut and pitched flat down on the cement floor, unconscious. The lads woke me up next morning, when it was still dark. "Tell us what happened!" Then I remembered what had happened

156

at the commandant's and told them. "How are we going to share out the grub?" the man in the bunk next to me asked, and his voice was trembling. "Equal shares all round," I told him. We waited till it got light. We cut up the bread and fat with a bit of thread. Each of us got a piece of bread about the size of a match-box, not a crumb was wasted. And as for the fat—well, of course, there was only enough to grease your lips with. But we parcelled it out, fair shares all round.

'Soon they put about three hundred of the strongest of us on draining a marsh, then off we went to the Ruhr to work in the mines. And there I stayed until 'forty-four. By that time our lads had knocked some of the stuffing out of Germany and the nazis had stopped looking down on us, prisoners. One day they lined us up, the whole day-shift, and some visiting *Oberleutnant* said through an interpreter, "Anyone who served in the army or worked before the war as a driver—one pace forward." About seven of us who'd been drivers before stepped out. They gave us some old overalls and took us under guard to Potsdam. When we got there, we were split up. I was detailed to work in "Todt". That was what the Germans called the set-up they had for building roads and defence works.

'I drove a German major of the engineers about in an Opel-Admiral. Now that was a real nazi hog for you! Short fellow with a pot-belly, as broad as he was tall, and a back-side on him as big as any wench's. He had three chins hanging down over his collar in front, and three whopping folds round his neck at the back. Must have carried a good hundredweight of pure fat on him, I should think. When he walked, he puffed like a steam-engine, and when he sat down to eat—hold tight! He'd go on all day, chewing and taking swigs from his flask of brandy. Now and then

157

I came in for a bit too. He'd stop on the road, cut up some sausage and cheese, and have a drink; and when he was in a good mood he'd toss me a scrap like to a dog. Never handed it to me. Oh, no, he considered that beneath him. But, be that as it may, there was no comparing it to the camp, and little by little I began to look like a man again. I even began to put on weight.

'For about two weeks I drove the major to and fro between Potsdam and Berlin, then he was sent to the front-line area to build defences against our troops. And then I gave up sleep. All night long I'd be thinking how to escape to my own side, my own country.

'We arrived in the town of Polotsk. At dawn, for the first time in two years I heard the boom of our artillery, and you can guess how my heart thumped at the sound. Why, mate, even when I first started courting Irina, it never beat like that! The fighting was going on east of Polotsk, about eighteen kilo-metres away. The Germans in the town were sore as hell, and jumpy, and my old pot-belly started drinking more and more. During the day-time we would drive round and he'd give instructions on how to build the fortifications, and at night he'd sit by himself drinking. He got all puffy, and there were great bags under his eyes.

'Well, I thought, no need to wait any longer, this is my chance. And I'm not going to escape alone, I've got to take old pot-belly with me, he'll come in useful over there!

'In a heap of rubble I found a heavy iron weight and wrapped a rag round it, so that if I had to hit him there wouldn't be any blood. I picked up a length of telephone wire in the road, got everything I needed ready, and hid it all under the front seat. One evening, two days before I said good-bye to the

158

Germans, I was on my way back from the filling station and I saw a German *Unter* staggering along blind drunk, grabbing at the wall. I pulled up, led him into a damaged building, shook him out of his uniform, and took his cap off his head. Then I hid the whole lot under the seat and I was ready.

'On the morning of June 29th, my major told me to take him out of town in the direction of Trosnitsa. He was in charge of some defences that were being built there. We drove off. The major was sitting on the back seat, taking a quiet doze, and I sat in front with my heart trying to jump out of my mouth. I drove fast, but outside the town I slowed down, then stopped and got out and had a look round; a long way behind there were two lorries coming on slowly. I got out my iron weight and opened the door wide. Old pot-belly was lying back on the seat, snoring as if he'd got his wife beside him. Well, I gave him a bang on the left temple with my iron. His head flopped on to his chest. I gave him another one, just to make sure, but I didn't want to kill him, I wanted to take him over alive. He was going to be able to tell our lads a lot of things. So I pulled the pistol out of his holster and shoved it in my pocket. Then I pushed a bracket down behind the back seat, tied the telephone wire round the major's neck and fastened it to the bracket. That was so he wouldn't tumble over on his side when I drove fast. I pulled on the German uniform and cap, and drove the car straight for the place where the earth was rumbling, where the fighting was.

'I ripped across the German front-line between two pillboxes. A bunch of submachine-gunners popped up out of a dug-out and I slowed down purposely so they would see I had a major with me. They started shouting and waving their arms to show me I mustn't go on, but I pretended not to understand and roared off at about eighty. Before they realized what was happening and opened fire I was on no man's land, weaving round the shell-holes no worse than a hare.

'There were the Germans firing from behind, and then our own chaps got fierce and had a smack at me from the front. Put four bullets through the wind-screen and riddled the radiator. But not far away I spotted a little wood near a lake, and some of our chaps running towards the car, so I drove into the wood and got out. Then I fell on the ground and kissed it. I could hardly breathe.

'A young fellow, with khaki shoulder-straps on his tunic I'd never seen before, reached me first and says with a grin, "Aha, you lousy Fritz, lost your way, eh?" I tore off my German tunic, threw the German cap down at my feet, and I says to him, "You lovely young kid. Sonny boy! Me a Fritz when I was born and bred in Voronezh! I was prisoner-of-war, see? And now unhitch that fat hog sitting in the car, take his briefcase and escort him to your commander." I handed over my pistol and was passed from one person to the next until evening when I had to report to the colonel in command of the division. By that time I had been fed and taken to the bath-house and questioned, and given a new uniform, so I went to the colonel's dug-out in proper order, clean in body and soul, and properly dressed. The colonel got up from his table, and came over to me, and in front of all the officers there, he kissed me and said, "Thank you, soldier, for the fine gift you brought us. Your major and his briefcase have told us more than any twenty Germans we might capture on the front-line. I shall recommend you for a decoration." His words and the affection he showed moved me so much I couldn't keep my lips from trembling, and all I could say was, "Comrade Colonel, I request to be enrolled in an infantry unit."

'But the colonel laughed and slapped me on the shoulder. "What kind of a fighter do you think you'd make when you can hardly stand on your feet? I'm sending you off to hospital straightaway. They'll patch you up there and put some food inside you, and after that you'll go home to your family for a month's leave, and when you come back to us, we'll think where to put you."

'The colonel and all the officers that were in the dug-out with him shook hands and said good-bye to me, and I went out with my head spinning because in the two years I'd been away I'd forgotten what it was like to be treated like a human being. And mind you, mate, it was a long time before I got out of the habit of pulling my head down into my shoulders when I had to talk to the high-ups, as if I was still scared of being hit. That was the training we got in those nazi camps.

'As soon as I got into hospital I wrote Irina a letter. I told her in a few words all about how I was taken prisoner and how I escaped with the German major. Just what made me boast like a kid, I couldn't tell you. Why, I couldn't even hold back from saying the colonel had promised to recommend me for a medal...

'For a couple of weeks I just slept and ate. They fed me a little at a time, but often; if they'd given me all the food I wanted, so the doctor said, I might have gone under. But after the two weeks were up, I couldn't look at food. There was no reply from home and, I must admit, I began to get mopy. Couldn't think of eating, sleep wouldn't come to me, and all kinds of bad thoughts kept creeping into my head. In the third week I got a letter from Voronezh. But it wasn't from Irina, it was from a neighbour of mine, a joiner. I wouldn't wish anyone to

161

get a letter like that. He wrote that the Germans had bombed the aircraft factory, and my cottage had got a direct hit with a heavy bomb. Irina and the girls were at home when it dropped. There was nothing left, he wrote, only a deep hole where the house had been... At first I couldn't finish reading that letter. Everything went dark before my eyes and my heart squeezed into a tight little ball so that I thought it would never open up again. I lay back on my bed and when I got a bit of strength back I read the letter to the end. My neighbour wrote that Anatoly was away in town during the bombing. He returned in the evening, took one look at the hole where his home had been, and went back to town the same night. All he told my neighbour, before he went, was that he was going to volunteer for the front.

'When my heart eased up and I heard the blood rushing in my ears, I remembered how Irina had clung to me when we parted at the station. That woman's heart of hers must have known all along we were not to see each other again in this world. And I had pushed her away... Once I had a family, a home of my own, it had all taken years to build, and it was all destroyed in a flash, and I was left all alone. It must be a dream, I thought, this messed-up life of mine. Why, when I had been a prisoner, nearly every night, of course, in my mind, I had talked to Irina and the kids, tried to cheer them up by promising them I'd come home and they mustn't cry. I'm tough, I said, I can stand it, we'll all be together again one day. For two years I had been talking to the dead!'

The big man was silent for a minute. When he spoke again, his voice faltered. 'Let's have a smoke, mate, I feel as if I was choking.'

We lighted up. The tapping of a wood-pecker sounded very loud in the flooded woodland. The

162

warm breeze still rustled the dry leaves of the alders, the clouds were still floating past in the towering blue, as though under taut white sails, but in those minutes of solemn silence the boundless world preparing for the great fulfilment of spring, for that eternal affirmation of the living in life, seemed quite different to me.

It was too distressing to keep silent and I asked, 'What happened then?'

'What happened then?' the story-teller responded reluctantly. 'Then I got a month's leave from the colonel, and a week later I was in Voronezh. I went on foot to the place where I had once lived with my family. There was a deep hole full of rusty water. The weeds all round came up to your waist. It was empty and still as a graveyard. I felt it bad then, mate, I can tell you! I stood there in sorrow, then I went back to the station. I wasn't there more than an hour altogether. I went back to the division the same day.

'But about three months later I did get a flash of joy, like a gleam of sunlight through the clouds. I got news of Anatoly. He sent me a letter from another front. He had got my address from that neighbour of mine. It seems he'd been to an artillery school to start with; his gift for mathematics stood him in good stead there. After a year he graduated with honours and went to the front, and now he wrote he had been promoted to captain, was commanding a battery of "forty-fives", and had been decorated six times. In a word, he'd left his old man far behind. And again I felt real proud of him. Say what you like, but my own son was a captain, and in command of a battery. That was something! And all those decorations too. It didn't matter that his dad was just carting shells and other stuff about in a Studebaker. His dad's time was past, but he, a captain,

163

had everything ahead of him.

'At nights now I began weaving an old man's dreams. When the war was over I'd get my son married and live with them. I'd do a bit of carpentry and look after the kiddies. I'd do all the kind of things an old man does. But that all went bust too. In the winter we went on advancing without a break and there wasn't time to write to each other very often, but towards the end of the war, right up near Berlin, I sent Anatoly a letter one morning and got an answer the very next day. It turned out that he and I had come up to the German capital by different routes and were now very close to each other. I could hardly wait for the moment when we'd meet. Well, the moment came... Right on the ninth of May, on the morning of Victory Day, my Anatoly was killed by a German sniper.

'The company commander sent for me in the afternoon. I saw there was a strange artillery officer sitting with him. I went into the room and he stood up as if he was meeting a senior. My C.O. said, "The lieutenant-colonel has come to see you, Sokolov," and turned away to the window. Something went through me like an electric shock. I knew there was trouble coming. The lieutenant-colonel came up to me and said, "Bear up, father. Your son, Captain Sokolov, was killed today at his battery. Come with me."

'I swayed, but I kept my feet. Even now it seems unreal the way that lieutenant-colonel and I drove in that big car along those streets strewn with rubble. I've only a foggy memory of the soldiers drawn up in line and the coffin covered with red velvet. But my Anatoly I saw as plain as I can see you now, mate. I went up to the coffin. Yes, it was my son lying there, and yet it wasn't. My son had been a lad, always smiling, with narrow shoulders and a sharp little Adam's apple sticking out of his thin neck, but here was a young broad-shouldered, full-grown man, and good-looking too. His eyes were half-closed as if he was looking past me into the far distance. Only the corners of his lips still had a bit of the smile my son used to have. The Anatoly I knew once. I kissed him and stepped aside. The lieutenant-colonel made a speech. My Anatoly's friends were wiping their tears, but I couldn't cry. I reckon the tears dried up in my heart. Perhaps that's why it still hurts so much.

'I buried my last joy and hope in that foreign German soil, the battery fired a volley to send off their commander on his long journey, and something seemed to snap inside me. When I got back to my unit I was a different man. Soon after that I was demobbed. Where was I to go? To Voronezh? Not for anything! I remembered I had a friend who had been invalided out of the army back in the winter and was living in Uryupinsk; he had asked me to come and live with him. So I went.

'My friend and his wife had no children. They lived in a cottage of their own on the edge of the town. He had a disability pension, but he worked as a driver in a lorry depot and I got a job there too. I settled with my friend and they gave me a home. We used to drive various loads about the suburbs and in the autumn we switched over to grain delivery work. It was then I got to know my new son, the one that's playing down there in the sand.

'First thing you'd do when you got back from a long trip would be to go to a café for a bite of something, and, of course, you'd put away a glass of vodka to get rid of your tiredness. It's a bad habit, but I had quite a liking for it by that time, I must admit. Well, one day I noticed this lad near the caf', and the next day I noticed him again. What a little ragamuffin he was! His face all smeared with water-melon juice and dust, dirty as anything, hair all over the place, but he'd got a pair of eyes like stars in the night sky, after it's been raining! And I grew so fond of him that, funny though it may seem, I started missing him, and I'd hurry to finish my run so I could get back to the caf' and see him sooner. That's where he got his food—he ate what people gave him.

'The fourth day I came in straight from the state farm with my lorry loaded with grain and pulled in at the caf'. There was my little fellow sitting on the steps, kicking his legs, and pretty hungry by the look of him. I poked my head out of the window and shouted to him, "Hi, Vanya! Come on, jump aboard, I'll give you a ride to the elevator, and then we'll come back here and have some dinner." My shout made him start, then he jumped down from the steps, scrambled on to the running board and pulled himself up to the window. "How do you know my name's Vanya?" he says quietly, and he opens those lovely eyes of his wide, waiting for my answer. Well, I told him I was just one of those chaps who know everything.

'He came round to the right side. I opened the door and let him in beside me, and off we went. Lively little fellow he was, but suddenly he got quiet, and started looking at me from under those long curly eyelashes of his, and sighing. Such a little fellow and he'd already learned to sigh. Was that the thing for him to be doing? "Where's your father, Vanya?" I asked. "He was killed at the front," he whispered. "And Mummy?" "Mummy was killed by a bomb when we were in the train." "Where were you coming from in the train?" "I don't know, I don't remem-ber..."   "And haven't you got any family at all?" "No, nobody." "But where do you sleep at night?" "Anywhere I can find."

166

'I felt the hot tears welling up inside me and I made up my mind at once. Why should we suffer alone and seperate like this! I'd take him in as my own son. And straightaway I felt easier in my mind and there was a sort of brightness there. I leaned over to him and asked, very quiet-like, "Vanya, do you know who I am?" And he just breathed it out, "Who?" And still as quiet, I says to him, "I'm your father."

'Lord alive, what happened then! He threw his arms round my neck, he kissed my cheeks, my lips, my forehead, and started hollering away like a little bird. Deafening it was, "Daddy dear! I knew it! I knew you'd find me! I knew you'd find me whatever happened! I've been waiting so long for you to find me!" He pressed himself to me and he was trembling all over, like a blade of grass in the wind. My eyes were misty and I was trembling, too, and my hands were shaking... How I managed to keep hold of the wheel I don't know. Even so I put her in the ditch and stopped the engine. While my eyes were so misty I was afraid to go, in case I knocked someone down. We sat there for about five minutes and my little son was still clinging to me for all he was worth, and not saying anything, just trembling all over. I put my right arm round him, hugged him gently, and turned the lorry round with my left hand and drove back to the cottage where I lived. I just couldn't go to the elevator after that.

'I left the lorry at the gate, took my new son in my arms and carried him into the house. And he got his little arms round my neck and hung on tight. He pressed his cheek to my unshaven chin and stuck there. And that's how I carried him in. My friend and his wife were both at home. I came in and winked at them with both eyes. Then, bold and cheerful, I said, "Well, I've found my little Vanya at last.

Here we are, good people." They hadn't got any children themselves and they both wanted a kid, so they guessed what was up straightaway and started bustling around. And the kid just wouldn't let me put him down. But I managed it somehow. I washed his hands with soap and sat him down at the table. My friend's wife ladled him out a plate of soup, and when she saw how he gulped it down, she just burst into tears. She stood at the stove, crying into her apron. And my Vanya, he saw she was crying, and he ran up to her, tugged at her skirt and said, "Why are you crying, Auntie? Daddy found me near the café. Everyone ought to be happy, and you are crying." But she only cried all the harder.

'After dinner I took him to the barber's to have his hair cut, and at home I gave him a bath myself in a tub and wrapped him up in a clean sheet. He hugged me tight and went to sleep in my arms. I laid him gently in bed, drove off to the elevator, unloaded the grain and took the lorry back to the depot. Then I went to the shops, I bought him a pair of serge trousers, a shirt, a pair of sandals and a straw cap. Of course, it all turned out to be the wrong size and no good for quality. My friend's wife gave me a ticking-off over the trousers. "Are you crazy," she says, "dressing a boy in serge trousers in heat like this!" And the next minute she had the sewing-machine on the table and was rummaging in the chest, and in an hour she had a pair of cotton shorts and a white shirt ready for my Vanya. I took him to bed with me and for the first time for many a night fell asleep peacefully. I woke up about four times in the night though. And there he was, nestling in the crook of my arm, like a sparrow under the eaves, breathing away softly. I can't find words to tell you what joy I felt. I'd try not to move, so as not to disturb him, but then I'd get up very quiet, light a match and just stand there, admiring him...

'Just before daybreak I woke. I couldn't make out why it seemed so stuffy. It was my young son. He'd climbed out of his sheet and was lying right across my chest, with his little foot on my throat. He's a rare young fidget to sleep with, he is; but I've got used to him. I miss him when he's not there. At night, I can stroke him while he's sleeping, I can smell his curls. It takes some of the pain out of my heart, makes it a bit softer. It had just about turned to stone, you know.

'At first he used to ride with me in the lorry, then I realized that that wouldn't do. After all, what do I need when I'm on my own? A hunk of bread and an onion with a pinch of salt will last a soldier the whole day. But with him it's different. Now you've got to get him some milk, now you've got to boil an egg for him, and he can't get along without something hot. But I had my work to do. So I plucked up my courage and left him in the care of my friend's wife. Well, he just cried all day, and in the evening ran away to the elevator to meet me. Waited there till late at night.

'I had a hard time with him at first. After one very tiring day we went to bed when it was still light. He used to be always chirruping like a sparrow, but this time he was very quiet. "What are you thinking about, son?" I asked. He just looked up at the ceiling. "What did you do with your leather coat, Daddy?" And I'd never had a leather coat in my life! I had to get round it somehow. "Left it in Voronezh," I told him. "And why were you so long looking for me?" So I said, "I looked for you, sonny, in Germany, in Poland, and all over Byelorussia, and you turned up in Uryupinsk." "Is Uryupinsk nearer than Germany? Is it far from our house to

Poland?" We went on talking like that till we dropped off to sleep.

'But do you think there wasn't a reason for his asking about that leather coat, mate? No, there was a reason behind it all right. It meant at some time or other his real father had worn a coat like that, and he had just remembered it. A kid's memory is like summer lightning, you know; it flashes and lights things up for a bit, then dies away. And that was how his memory worked, like the flashes of summer lightning.

'We might have gone on living another year in Uryupinsk together, but in November I had an accident. I was driving along a muddy road through a village and I went into a skid. There happened to be a cow in the way and I knocked it over. Well, you know how it is—the women raised a hullabaloo, a crowd gathered, and soon there was a traffic inspector on the spot. I asked him to go easy, but he took my licence away. The cow got up, stuck its tail in the air and went galloping away down the street, but I lost my licence. I went through the winter as a joiner, and then got in touch with an old army friend—he works as a driver in your district—and he invited me to come and stay with him. You can do joinery work for a year, he says, then you can get a new licence in our region. So now my son and I, we're on the march to Kashary.

'But even if I hadn't had that accident with the cow, you know, I'd have left Uryupinsk just the same, I can't stay in one place for long. When my Vanya gets older and he's got to go to school, I expect I'll knuckle under and settle down. But for the time being we're tramping the Russian land together.'

'Does he get tired?' I asked.

'Well, he doesn't go far on his own feet; most of

170

the time he rides on me. I hoist him on to my shoulder and carry him. When he wants to stretch his legs, he jumps down and runs about at the side of the road, prancing around like a little goat. No, it's not that, mate, we'd get along all right. The trouble is my heart's got a knock in it somewhere, ought to have a piston changed. Sometimes it gives me such a stab I nearly get a black-out. I'm afraid one day I may die in my sleep and frighten my little son. And that's not the only thing. Nearly every night I see the dear ones I've lost in my dreams. And mostly it's as if I was behind barbed wire and they were on the other side, at liberty. I talk about everything to Irina and the children, but as soon as I try to pull the barbed wire apart, they go away, seem to melt before my eyes. And there's another funny thing about it. In the daytime I always keep a firm grip on myself, you'll never get a sigh out of me. But sometimes I wake up at night and my pillow's wet through.'

From the river came the sound of my friend's voice and the splash of oars in the water.

This stranger, who now seemed a close friend of mine, held out his big hand, firm as a block of wood.

'Good-bye, mate, good luck to you!'

'Good luck and a good journey to Kashary!'

'Thanks. Hey, sonny, let's go to the boat.'

The boy ran to his side, took hold of the corner of his jacket and started off with tiny steps beside his striding father. Two orphans, two grains of sand swept into strange parts by the tremendous hurricane of war... What did the future hold for them? I wanted to believe that this Russian, this man of unbreakable will, would stick it out, and that the boy would grow at his father's side into a man who could endure anything, overcome any obstacle if his country called upon him to do so.

I felt sad as I watched them go. Perhaps all would have been well at our parting if Vanya, after going a few paces, had not twisted round on his stumpy legs and waved to me with his little rosy hand. And suddenly a soft but taloned paw seemed to grip my heart, and I turned hastily away. No, not only in their sleep do they weep, these elderly men whose hair turned grey in the years of war. They weep in their waking hours, too. The thing is to be able to turn away in time. The main thing is not to wound a child's heart, not to let him see the unwilling tear that burns the cheek of a man.

1957

REQUEST TO READERS

Raduga Publishers would be glad to have your opinion of this book, its translation and design and any suggestions you may have for future publications. Please send all your comments to 17, Zubovsky Boulevard, Moscow, USSR.

Перевод сделан по изданию:
М. Шолохов. Собр. соч. в 8-ми тт.
Изд-во "Правда", 1975 г.

Редактор
Н. КОЧАРОВА

Художники
Б. АЛИМОВ, П. НИКИПОРЕЦ

Художественный редактор
Е. ПОЛИКАШИН

Технический редактор
В. ГУНИНА